GLOUCESTERSHIRE
GHOST
TALES

GLOUCESTERSHIRE GHOST TALES

ANTHONY NANSON &
KIRSTY HARTSIOTIS

The
History
Press

First published 2015

The History Press
The Mill, Brimscombe Port
Stroud, Gloucestershire, GL5 2QG
www.thehistorypress.co.uk

British Library Cataloguing in Publication Data.
A catalogue record for this book is available from the British Library.

ISBN 978 0 7509 6367 1

Typesetting and origination by The History Press
Printed in Great Britain

CONTENTS

Acknowledgements

We wish to acknowledge the sources listed in the bibliography and the links in the chain by which the stories reached those publications. Where possible we've drawn on multiple sources for each story here retold. Many thanks to Jessica Douglas-Home, Ann Hettich and Jill Watson of the Chipping Campden History Society, Mark Howe, Katy Jordan, Laura Kinnear, Glenn Smith, David Wilkinson, Newent Storytellers, Bath Storytelling Circle, Stroud Story Supper, Stroud Out Loud, Bristol Central Library, Cheltenham Local Studies Library, Gloucestershire Archives, Stroud Library, and Hopewell Colliery Museum. Special thanks to Katherine Soutar for her stunning cover artwork and to The History Press for commissioning this book and sending us on this journey together. The line illustrations are by Kirsty Hartsiotis.

MAP OF THE STORIES

TEWKESBURY ■

⑬ ④

⑮

NEWENT ■

⑥

STOW ■ ⑲

CHELTENHAM ■

⑦

③

⑳ GLOUCESTER ■

⑩

⑨

STROUD ■

② ⑱

CIRENCESTER ■

⑭

⑤

⑧

⑯

■

⑪

① CHIPPING SODBURY ■

⑰ ⑫
■
BRISTOL

The numbers on the map refer to the numbering of the stories.

INTRODUCTION

The ghost story is one of the most living of folk tale genres. People remain fascinated by the ghosts of their locality, their family, even the building they live in. Start telling ghost stories and you can be at it all night, since so many people have an experience to relate or a story they've heard. When you listen to ghost stories the world suddenly becomes a more unnerving place.

Gloucestershire, like other counties, is blessed with many books of ghost stories. These useful gazetteers present the tales in summary form in order to provide comprehensive coverage. Some of the stories involve a convoluted sequence of events, but most are simple sightings of a particular manifestation, whether a report from one person or a recurring account of the kind that folklorists call a 'local legend'.

Many people believe that ghosts are real, and calling a story a 'legend' doesn't preclude the possibility that it may recount something that really happened. One of the characteristics of legends of all kinds – whether you're talking about Robin Hood, or a healing well, or big cats stalking the Forest of Dean – is that they *are* believed to be true, at least when they originate, and uncertainty about how much they represent real events may endure indefinitely. So it is with ghosts.

Such reports and legends are one kind of 'ghost story'. But there's another kind: the literary ghost stories popularised by the likes of Sheridan Le Fanu, Algernon Blackwood, and M.R. James. These stories are framed as fiction rather than truth and also differ from local ghost legends in being more elaborate, more fully imagined stories that are carefully crafted to entertain – and to scare! But you can't completely separate these two categories; writers of literary ghost stories have often drawn inspiration from folklore.

In this book we've selected twenty Gloucestershire ghost stories from the hundreds gathered in the gazetteers, and reshaped them as fully dramatised stories that we hope are both enjoyable on the page and also well structured for oral retelling. Our choice of stories came down, ultimately, to those which most caught our imagination, though we've tried to provide a good spread of geography, theme, and of gloomier as well as more cheerful tales. Bristol is included because it was originally in Gloucestershire. The book is a companion to Anthony's *Gloucestershire Folk Tales*, so we've avoided repeating the six ghost stories included in that volume: 'Betty's Grave', 'White Lady's Gate', 'The Lady of the Mist', 'The King's Revenge', 'The Price of a Lawyer's Soul', and 'Puesdown Inn'.

Ghost stories usually have a 'back story', about the circumstances that brought the ghost into being, and a 'front story' concerning encounters with the ghost. One challenge in crafting a ghost story is the relationship between front and back story. Sometimes the back story predominates, till the tale concludes with a 'ghost ex machina'. Other stories focus on the front story, keeping the back story mysterious or embedding it as a story within a story. Yet others have a more complex dynamic between these two elements. Field visits to the geographical locations that feature in the stories have vitally inspired our shaping of the stories and helped us evoke a sense of place. Because of the imaginative liberties we've taken with the stories, we've fictionalised any real individuals in them who may still be alive, including by changing their names.

The story motifs found in Gloucestershire's ghost stories are similar to those in other English counties, whether they be white ladies, poltergeists, haunted barrows, or phantom monks, so it's difficult to generalise about local tendencies. Most ghost stories involve personal tragedies or moments of intense emotion. However, ghosts are notably associated with major social upheavals, and we tentatively note the prominence of the Civil War and the Dissolution of the Monasteries in Gloucestershire ghostlore. These were national events, of course, but of special importance in Gloucestershire because Gloucester held out as a Parliamentarian stronghold throughout the Civil War and because of the large number of religious houses in the county.

In the end, ghost stories are about death. This is the reason for their fascination. In a scientific age, in which the supernatural is banished from most aspects of life, local ghost stories make connections between the landscapes and townscapes we inhabit and our nervous speculations about what happens to us when we die.

Anthony Nanson and Kirsty Hartsiotis, 2015

1

THE WHITE LADY OF OVER COURT

That year, 1937, the carol-playing at Almondsbury happened to fall on 17 December. When the members of the Easter Compton Prize Band carried their instruments up the drive of Over Court, there was much joking about whether they'd see the 'White Lady'. John Purnell knew all about the legend. He was only fourteen, but he'd been coming to Over Court on carol night since he was a little lad. This was the first time, though, they'd carolled on the fateful 17 December. Mr Young's lantern made little impression on the undergrowth each side of the drive and John couldn't help nervously glancing into the shadows.

For Micky Merrett, it was his first visit to Over Court. He was new to the area and new to the band and only two years older than John – so the old hands were directing most of their joking at him: 'Maybe there'll be a fine lady for you tonight, young Micky. It could be your lucky night.'

They trooped under the archway of the clock tower and followed the way round to the main door of the grand old gabled mansion. Four hundred years old the place was, though there was said to have been a yet older house before it. The band lined themselves up on the gravel. The full moon gleamed on their instruments as they raised them to their lips. Over Court usually gave the biggest donation of the night, so they performed three whole carols and gave them all the puff they had.

The third number was 'Hark the Herald Angels Sing'. They were on the third verse when John Purnell, as he played his cornet, found his eyes drawn along the building to a tree near the left-hand corner. The shadows were very deep under the tree, but there was something there; something pale, tall, slender, its shape hard to make out in the chiaroscuro of moonlight and shadow. John couldn't tell whether it was, or was not, a human figure. It seemed too tall. Yet today was 17 December, the very date when the White Lady was said to rise from her pond!

He turned his eyes back to the family listening in the doorway. His fingers made a few duff notes. When he glanced again at the tree the white form had gone.

The musicians finished the carol, collected the money, and trudged back along the drive. The men were still joking about the White Lady, blithely unaware of what John had seen. He kept quiet. There'd be no end to the ribbing if they heard that he thought he'd seen the ghost. There had to be another explanation. Previous years, he'd seen deer on the estate, some very pale, almost white. If a deer rose on its hind legs to browse a higher branch, it would make a tall slender figure. Could that be what he'd seen?

If he told anyone, it would be the new lad, Micky. Right now Micky was at the front of the jumble of men and instruments filing through the archway and John was at the back. It was just when John was under the archway that Mr Young's lantern went out. The men at the front came to an abrupt halt and everyone went silent. There was a faint shushing of wind in the treetops, the distant call of an owl.

Micky's half-broken voice called out in a hoarse stage whisper, 'There, through the gap!'

John wormed through the press of men just in time to see what everyone else saw. In the dark space between two trees to the left of the drive was a figure, caught by slivers of creamy moonlight, that seemed to radiate a blue glow. She seemed tall because of the conical headdress she wore and because she appeared to be floating several inches above the ground. Her long gown concealed her feet and from the headdress fell the gossamer blur of a veil. Despite this

elegance of attire, she moved with erratic staggers. The whole band watched, electrified, as the figure zigzagged, stumbling and lurching, through the undergrowth and trees, heading back towards the gardens, until it disappeared through a hedge and all they could see were the shadows.

They stood there in silence for some time, till at last old Ted Robbins declared, 'Well, I'll be damned!'

The men looked awkwardly at each other. No joking now. They'd seen the White Lady! All of them had. It couldn't have been a trick of the light if they'd all seen her. The Christmas cheer had gone out of them. They'd seen a ghost, for one thing. But they knew the story too; they knew why she was staggering like that. It's easy to joke about a tragedy that happened hundreds of years ago – if it happened at all. It's something else when you've seen the ghost of a murdered woman with your own eyes.

Surely there was a rational explanation, but none of them could think what it might be. They trudged sombrely up the lane to the other houses where they had to play. Their playing was lacklustre, to say the least.

Only Micky Merrett didn't know the legend, but he was keen now to hear it and so old Ted told him it.

'No one knows how many hundred years back it happened. There were a great lord as lived in the big house, though whether it were that house there now or another one afore, I can't say. This lord had a lady and she were as beautiful as they come. Like any man with a beautiful wife, he were jealous of her beauty. He were a fair bit older too, as were normal back then, and he treated her like he owned her. Normal it may have been, but the natural feelings of the yuman heart will be as they be. The lady fell in love with a likely lad from the village. He were not so high-born as she, but he were close to her age and lusty and kind, and that's what counted.

'They tried to be circumspect, as you might say, about when and where they met. It had to be when the lord of the manor were away on high matters of property and Crown. There came a time when he'd went far away, or so the lady thought, and weren't due back till Christmas Eve. It were a moonlit night like tonight, that 17 December, as she sent for her chap to come to the house. Foolhardy, you might say, but the servants loved her all right, they wouldn't tell on her, so maybe it were better him coming there than her traipsing round the village by night. I daresay it were also a sight more comfortable in her chamber than anywhere else they could go.

'They never got as far as her chamber. She received him in the hallway, dressed up proper fine to please him. A bonny sight she were. But suddenly there was hoof beats outside. It all happened so quick. The young Casanova were holding the lady in his arms when her husband – back too soon – come through the door. He takes in the situation in a glance. He pulls out his sword. I reckon as he meant to kill the usurper. Maybe the lady rushed forward to stop him, to try and protect her sweetheart. The point of the sword took her in the side and the blood spilled down her dress.

'What happened to the young man, the story don't say, only that the lady fled from the house and through the grounds, staggering from the wound, till she come to the fishpond. I warrant she didn't see it in the darkness. In she went with a great splash. The weed entangled her limbs and her hair. Her waterlogged dress dragged her down. She were already weak from losing so much blood. And so she drowned. It were the 17 December, like today, and they say that every 17 December she do rise again from that pond.'

Neither John Purnell nor Micky Merrett could sleep that night. They met up as soon as it was light and went back to the place in front of the clock tower where they'd seen the apparition. The place seemed very different in the daylight, more ordinary. Hard to credit what they'd seen. Maybe it had just been a trick of the darkness and moonlight. Maybe it had been some posh lass from the house in fancy dress who'd had too much sherry.

They worked out the route the apparition had gone through the undergrowth towards the gardens, and tried to follow it. They ducked under branches, pushed between bushes, but the branches and stems were too impenetrable to even get to the hedge. So they gave that up and went back down the drive and found another way around the hedge. They were trespassing, of course, but they were used to that. They carried on in roughly the direction they'd seen her go, till – voila – they came to a pond.

'This must be it!' cried John.

'*The* pond?' said Micky.

'Must be. She must've come this way after she was stabbed. Maybe the husband was after her and she had to keep going.'

'But why go through the undergrowth instead of on the drive?'

John shrugged. 'The way she was dressed, what old Ted said … it was hundreds and hundreds of years ago. The house, the paths, everything would be different.'

Yes, thought John, they must have seen a vision of her flight to the pond. But what about the first pale figure he'd seen by the far corner of the house? That wouldn't fit with this route. He stared at the murky olive water. The story said that on 17 December the White Lady *rose* from the pond. He pictured the dead woman rising up, water streaming from her gown and veil, to lurch back to the house to repeat yet again her last desperate journey from house to pond. He stared again through the still, smooth surface of water, saw the tangled labyrinth of weed, a shimmy of movement – and there, in the murk, glimpsed the hollow eyes and pallid skin of a grave young face staring back at him.

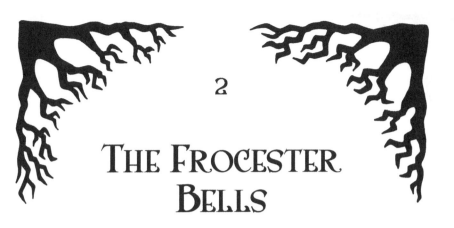

2

THE FROCESTER
BELLS

'Look, that sign says Eastington and Frocester,' said Martin Adams. 'I was born at Frocester, you know. Haven't been back for years. Mind if we have a look?'

Sandra was tired; it had been a long day, and there was still a way to go. The A38 had already seemed interminable. But Martin was so keen, so she smiled and said, no, she didn't mind.

Excitedly he showed her the house where he'd been born, the pub where his dad had liked a drink, the big house. It didn't take long, but by the time they were done the sun was casting a pink glow into the western sky.

'There's one more thing.' Martin caught her hand and grinned. 'But we'll have to drive there.'

Back into the Triumph Vitesse they got, and Martin drove them past the little church down a road signposted 'Coaley'. After a short way, another church tower appeared, silhouetted against the sunset.

They pulled up by the lychgate and Sandra got out and looked around. It seemed the middle of nowhere. On the other side of the road a low, wooded hill rose up a couple of fields away. On this side the dark shape of the tower reared above the hedge.

'Come on!' cried Martin.

Sandra wondered why his voice was so full of glee. As soon as she was through the lychgate, she stopped. There was the tower, but it stood all alone, with just the shell of a little building opposite – a porch maybe? In the middle, where the church should have been, was nothing but a raised rectangle of grass. Sandra shuddered and drew her shawl tighter over her dress. The absence of a church looked horribly wrong, like a gaping wound.

'Where's the church?' she cried.

Martin skipped up the steps on to the grass and danced about, his bell-bottoms flapping around his legs.

'They knocked it down almost twenty years ago, in '54. I remember that. There was an archaeological dig and everything.'

That made sense, Sandra supposed. The graveyard didn't look abandoned, exactly. There were fresh flowers on some of the graves. But the place looked so strange, that tower looming there by itself in the dying light.

'Why did they leave it like this?' she asked.

'Don't know. Even the bells are gone. My dad told me they gave them to Eastington.'

Sandra's eye caught a movement by the tower. Standing in the tower's shadow was a woman in a long stiff black dress. Sandra's heart began to thump. She realised the woman was staring right at her. She could see her white face clearly, and it was full of fury. There was something not right about the woman, that strange dress, like a costume out of a play. Martin seemed oblivious. Sandra stared back at the woman – and as she did she felt a rush of something – anger? evil? – hit her like a punch in the stomach. It roiled over her as she held the woman's gaze, and bile rose in her mouth.

She wrenched her gaze away. 'Martin!'

He turned, but in that instant the woman had gone. Sandra was shaking uncontrollably. When Martin asked her what was wrong she shook her head and walked back to the car. She was so silent that instead of going back to the A38 he drove on to Coaley, stopped the car at the Fox and Hounds, and bought them each a pint of cider. Sandra drank her cider, and by the end of the pint she had a ghost of a smile on her face, but she wouldn't tell Martin what she'd seen, not then, and not ever.

❖ ❖ ❖

A couple of hundred years before, the four bell-ringers from Coaley Church were sitting in the exact same corner of the pub where Martin and Sandra sat in 1973. They'd been there all evening, supping cider, laughing, and quietly talking. When the landlord rang the bell and they filed out they saw Coaley Church tower lit up by the full moon. They smiled at each other, emboldened by the cider.

'Tonight be the night, lads,' said Tom Workman.

Quickly and quietly, they made their way round the back of the church to where Tom's cart and placid old donkey, Betty, were waiting. John Griffin stowed a small barrel of cider on the cart, 'for emergencies' he said, and off they set.

It was a short and easy journey under the full moon. The tower of Frocester Church soon loomed above them. They led the donkey into the silent churchyard, then looked up at the church. It was a sorry sight: the roof fallen in, the glass gone from half the windows, and bats flitting in and out.

'Serve they right, it do,' said Tom, 'allowing him to get like this!'

The tower door was hanging open. Cracked stone steps spiralled up into darkness. The men lit their rushlights, stepped over the weeds and crumbled masonry on the floor, and slowly made their way up the stairs. The rushlights' leaping shadows only seemed to enlarge the darkness as they groped their way up. At last, after what seemed an eternity, Jimmy Webb banged his head on the bell loft's floor.

'Ow!'

He fumbled open the hatch, and moonlight streamed through. Staring up they saw the dark shapes of a ring of six bells. Jimmy, the smallest and nimblest, shinned up into the loft.

'They be all rung down, lads,' he said. 'This nearest one will do. It be over the hatch already.' The bell was nearly as big as Jimmy. 'We can allus come back for the others.'

While Jimmy clambered around the bell cage to hook the rope over the beam above, the others muffled the bell by stuffing their jackets inside it. John scrambled up after Jimmy to help take the weight of the bell as Jimmy carefully detached its own rope and attached the one they'd brought. At Jimmy's soft cry of 'Ready!' the two in the loft braced their grip on the rope against the bell's weight. 'Oof!' Tom and William Prout, the fourth member of the party, sagged under the weight as the bell was lowered down to them. Jimmy's and John's arm muscles bulged as they held it steady.

'Down he goes!'

Steadily they lowered it down until they had it balanced on the stairs ready to carry down.

'Good piece of work, lads!' cried Tom. 'Now let's get him downstairs.'

It was a tight squeeze, and manoeuvring the heavy bell after several pints of cider was a logistical challenge. No one had a free hand for the rushlights, so William positioned them at strategic points on the stairs. With quite a bit of scraping and dinging and a lot of swearing, they managed to get the bell to a small landing halfway down.

'Let's stop a minute, lads,' said Tom, and they gently lowered the bell to the floor.

William, who was a clerk by trade and the most learned of the party, picked up the rushlight he'd left there and squinted at the bell.

'There's some writing here.' He rubbed at the filthy bell metal with his sleeve. '"W. Whitmore 1639", it says.' He scrubbed some more. 'Then some numbers … and … maybe another name. Can't read it, though.'

'Whitmore'll be the bell-maker,' said John, giving it a ding. 'Fine old bell – but strange how he do glitter, don't ye think?'

The others looked, and saw by the rushlight that the bell did indeed sparkle with an unearthly light. The tower seemed to get darker. It suddenly seemed a good time to nip down to the cart for some liquid fortification.

It was a merry crew that made their way back to the bell, but when they got there they stopped dead. Sitting right on top of the bell was an old lady in a stiff black dress. She was looking straight at them with fury in her eyes.

'Hell's bells!' cried Tom. 'Where did her come from?'

Jimmy said, 'It be like my old granny. Her used to wander off at night and didn't know where her was to. I reckons as this old biddy do belong at Downton Farm. We best take her back there when we're done. Come on, granny, get down off the bell!'

The old lady wouldn't budge. The more they cajoled, the angrier she looked. When they took to taunting, the fury on her face would have scared the Devil – but not four bell-ringers high on cider.

'There yent nothing for it,' said Tom. 'We'll have to move the bell with her on him.'

The four men positioned themselves around the bell and *heaved*. It wouldn't shift. It was like it was stuck fast to the floor, and the old woman stuck fast to it. They tried every way they could to lift the bell, and every word they could think of to persuade the old woman off it, but neither she nor the bell would budge. So they trooped back down the stairs for another fortifying drink.

'Let's at least move the donkey and cart closer to the tower,' said John.

When they tried to lead old Betty closer she bucked and kicked until she was free of the traces, then ran to stand, shivering, by the gate.

Tom scratched his head. 'Her yent usually no trouble,' he said. 'Oh well, one last go.'

They piled up the stairs again, and there was the old besom still sitting on the bell, still glaring. But as William held the rushlight high they noticed something strange. They could see the stones of the tower right through the old woman. It dawned on them one by one that this was not some old biddy from the farm but something else entirely.

They bolted back down the stairs, hooked the donkey up to the cart, and they and the donkey ran all the way home to Coaley.

You would think that, after that, they wouldn't want to sup cider again anytime soon, yet the very next night they were fortifying themselves once more at the Fox and Hounds. As they drank, the story came spilling out.

Most of the regulars laughed at their tale, but there was one who didn't. He wasn't a Coaley man; he was from Frocester, had married a Coaley girl and come to her farm to live.

'I reckon as I know what was going on,' he said. 'They do say that, more'n a hundred years back, there was an old woman in Frocester as gave the money to some bell-founder to make a bell – and that right at the last moment she brought her jewels to throw into the molten metal, to make the bell special-like.'

The four bell-ringers went white.

'So that's why the bell was sparkly,' cried William. 'It was those jewels in it.'

The Frocester man nodded. 'I reckon it was her as you met, still protecting her bell after all these years. With the likes of you bell thieves about, I reckon she'll be a-haunting that church for many years to come.'

3

'SAVE ME TONIGHT FROM BENHALL'S DREARY WOOD'

There was a carter who lived in Cheltenham when it was a smaller town than today, scarcely bigger than a village. Abed one night in his cottage, the carter had a dream. He saw the face and form of a woman who seemed to be in his bedroom, sitting in his own bed, and yet seemed not to be. Through her lank black hair, through the weary lines of her face, through her thread-bare shift, he could see the texture of the wall beyond. She was pleading to him, 'Save me tonight from Benhall's dreary wood.'

Well, dreams are dreams. They seem intense at the time but fade with the coming of dawn. The next day, the carter drove a load of malt to Gloucester, then headed back to Cheltenham with bags of coal from the Forest. Much of the day was wasted waiting for the coal to be loaded, so it was already dark by the time he came back through Benhall Wood. Only tiny slivers of woodland remain there today, but back in those days Benhall Wood was a dense dark expanse, with a tangle of nettles and brambles beneath the trees. After nightfall you could hear nightingales, foxes' barks, the sudden flutter of bats, and there were desperate men who lived in the wood who had no roof of their own.

So it was a surprise to see at such an hour a woman standing alone on the roadside. The carter's impulse would normally be to stay on his cart and keep the horses moving, slow trudge that they managed with that weight of coal. But there was something so forlorn about this woman as she glanced up at him. The memory of his dream flashed into his mind, though it was too faint, and the moonlight too dim, for him to measure any similarity save that the hair showing below the woman's bonnet was dark.

He brought the cart to a standstill. 'Everything all right, mistress?' Only now did he see that she was heavily pregnant.

'I'm meeting someone near here. He told me to follow the path from behind the charcoal burners' pile.'

She indicated the smoking pile of wood and earth. Her hand, he noticed, trembled.

'You've walked all the way from Cheltenham?'

'I have, sir. He told me to come after dark; but I set off a bit earlier while there was still some light.'

'"He" being your husband?'

She gave a diffident shrug. 'Not yet my husband. He said as we shall go to a house he has in Leicestershire and there be wed.'

In spite of his caution the carter got down from his seat. The woman's face, seen closer, did seem familiar. He thought again of his dream. 'Save me tonight from Benhall's dreary wood,' the dream-woman had begged.

He said, 'So it's to go away and get married that you've come to meet him in the wood?'

'Aye,' she breathed, and you could see what a strain it was for her even to stand there with the weight of the child in her womb. 'He said the place isn't far in the wood, but I do confess I feel afraid.'

What kind of man would expect a woman in her condition to walk all this way? The carter considered the situation. It was possible this lass could be the decoy of a ruffian waiting in the shadows. The coal was one thing, but if he lost his horses and cart as well he would be truly shafted. But to use a pregnant woman for such a caper?

'Would you like me to come with you?' he said at last.

'I don't mean to put you to any trouble like,' she said, but it was plain his offer was welcome.

He followed her along the dark path, twisting and turning among the trees, the way lit only by the faint grey moonlight piercing the branches. Brambles snagged at the woman's skirts. She toiled with the weight of the child. When she stumbled the carter steadied her.

Ahead they heard the sound of a spade striking the earth. The path opened into a small clearing where a man in shirtsleeves was digging a hole in the ground. A mound of earth stood beside him. The hole was long and narrow. At the crunch of their footsteps the man looked sharply up.

'Milly —' The words died on his lips when he saw she was not alone. He had a foxy look: eyes close together, sharp lips and nose; his hair might possibly have been red. In that frozen moment all three of them took in the situation. Looming larger than all else was the hole the man had dug; a hole as long as the woman was tall and just wide enough to fit her swollen belly; a hole dark and dank, a black void in the earth, where wriggling worms waited, where the weight of shovelled-in soil would hold you tight and still for ever.

Then two things happened in the same breath. The woman fainted. The man dropped his spade and fled. Away through the trees he went, crunch, crunch, crunch, and he was gone.

The carter knelt by the fallen woman and lifted her head on his lap and brushed the dirt and dead leaves from her hair.

Feebly she moaned as she came round. 'He was going to … that hole … O Lord! … I knew he didn't really want my baby …'

When she was ready the carter helped her back to the cart on the road. He heaved her on to the seat and sat up beside her to drive her into town. She was distraught from what had happened, what the man she thought had loved her had been plotting to do; but her grief about that was soon overtaken by her body's imperatives. Maybe it was the shock that brought it on, or the fall when she'd fainted, or the bumpy cart ride. Her waters broke as they reached the edge of town. She had no family in Cheltenham, it wasn't her home town, so he took her to his own cottage and laid her on his bed. There was no woman in his life to help. He gave a penny to a lad in the street to fetch a midwife. It was a long and loud night. Not long after the sun had risen over the chimney pots the baby was born.

All the rest of that day Milly stayed in the carter's bed while the midwife fussed about and the baby was passed back and forth between the mother's breast and a makeshift cradle. At the day's end the carter made up a bed for himself on the floor downstairs. When the midwife had gone home he came up to check the mother and child had everything they required.

The woman reached out her hands to him and clasped his hand in both of hers. 'Thank you, sir. Thank you. Truly you saved me last night in Benhall's dreary wood.'

As she spoke, the memory of his dream returned. He realised that the lighting of the room was exactly as it had been in the dream, and so was the way the woman looked – the lank black hair, the weary lines of her face, the threadbare shift. For a few heartbeats the memory of the dream merged with the flesh and blood of the woman before him, as if the two were one and the spirit of the woman who would have died last night was appearing to him here and now as this woman warm and living clasped his hand with gratitude and her baby gurgled in its cot.

4

LADY JULIANA'S VAULT

The moon was only a sliver in the sky, but it was enough to light the truncated drive up to the ruins of Old Campden House in Chipping Campden. The night was still, but in St James's churchyard the tall conifers and boxy yews crackled with a dark energy. The moonlight touching the yellowy stone of the church turned it into a melange of shadow and silvery highlight. An owl hooted. From the shadow of the south wall came a figure that seemed to catch the moonlight inside itself. Glowing softly from within, it glided across the churchyard. It didn't stop to pass around the gravestones, but drifted silently through them, till it came to a part of the churchyard wall where the stone rose to a pointed apex denoting a blocked gateway.

A moment later the figure appeared, still glowing faintly, on the other side and glided up the drive. Away from the trees the moonlight shone more brightly and the figure was revealed as a bent old woman in a dark gown making her way to the ruins. One pier remained of the grand doorway. The empty mullioned windows gaped at the star-spangled sky.

She didn't turn to look at the gatehouse towers, but, as she passed, a curtain was twitched aside in the right-hand tower and two faces pressed against the glass.

'Told you! She's there again!' husked one in a stage whisper.

'Lady Juliana's walking … Woooo!' whispered back the other, lifting her arms in imitation of a ghost.

The curtain snapped suddenly shut and the two children started as their mother loomed over them.

'You come away from there! That bent for the likes of you to see. Them Artsy-Craftsy folk, meddling in things they shunt've! They come in, a-knowing nothing of us and ourn, and now that poor man is dead and *she* be a-walking again as was resting quiet since afore I were born.'

The moon slipped behind a cloud and the drive fell into darkness. The ghost of Lady Juliana Noel glided on, lost in a world long past. She stands on the terrace of the fine house, many chimneyed, with rows of mullioned windows and a classical arched door, that her father, Sir Baptist Hicks, built in 1612. She feels the hot sticky grasp of her small son's hand and gives it a squeeze. There's laughter all around and she sees the bright skirts and doublets of the assembled party coming back along the terrace walk from dessert at the banqueting house ... Her son's hand slips away and it's more than thirty years later, the end of the Civil War. She is tight-lipped with fury, staring at the ruins, the yellow stone burnt pink, the piles of rubble. She hears someone say, 'It was Prince Rupert's orders ...' and her anger almost overwhelms her. To think that the King's men did this, when her husband gave up his life for King Charles's cause! She hears herself say, 'They will pay!'... Then she's feeling the aches of age in her bones, fourteen years gone by, as she listens to the report that her steward, William Harrison, was murdered ... sees the scaffold with its burdens, the old man and woman, the idiot son, and the anger rises again ... She sees Harrison very plainly alive, two years later, head bowed as he stands in her hall in Court House, her father's old stables, muttering his wondrous tale of pirates and slavery in Turkey ... Another twenty years and still clinging to life, too stubborn to let go despite the pain and the longing for rest ... A rest that has again been disturbed ...

'It may go all the way down,' said Norman Jewson, Arts and Crafts architect, as he examined the chancel arch in St James's Church. He stared at the pier rising up to the low Perpendicular arch. The cracks in the pier were very obvious. 'It's possible there's subsidence in the vault. We'll have to take a look.' He glanced at his friend Fred Griggs, the etcher and fellow member of the Society for the Protection of Ancient Buildings, who'd come along as town representative.

'We can't lose this beautiful church,' agreed Griggs.

The new vicar was nodding too. 'We'll need permission from Lord Gainsborough to enter his vault. I'll write the letter straight away.'

The three men shook hands and, beaming, went on their way. It was clear they thought this morning's investigation a job well done; but the church sexton, Harry Withers, shook his head. Open the Gainsborough Vault? He eyed the black-columned tomb and white marble effigies of Sir Baptist Hicks and his wife, then nervously raised his eyes to Lady Juliana's tall marble form. Her stare seemed as blank as ever, but was something flickering there …?

Withers was old enough to remember when Mr Haines had opened the vault, back in – what? – 1881? He remembered the death that had followed and how he'd sneaked into the gatehouse garden and on to the drive of the old ruins to seek a glimpse of Lady Juliana walking. He never saw her, thank the Lord! And hadn't old Lord Gainsborough died that year as well, *and* the daughter he'd disinherited for marrying beneath herself? He shook his head again. If that Mr Jewson and Mr Griggs said the church might fall down, then surely it was a good thing to fix it. He glanced up at Lady Juliana again. Was that a glint in those blank marble eyes? Withers shivered and told himself he was imagining things.

Permission was granted and the current Lord Gainsborough sent an agent to observe the work. A mason raised the floor to open up the vault. Withers, the vicar, Jewson, and the agent lined up to go down. A dank smell rose out of the opening, carrying ancient damp and … something else. Withers' heart was pounding. He watched helplessly as the agent and the vicar went down. When the architect was about to follow them Withers could bear it no longer and grabbed the man's sleeve.

'You do know what they say, sir,' he began.

Jewson said he didn't and looked confused, foreigner that he was – they said he came from Norfolk before he settled near Cirencester.

'They says as one of us four will be dead within a week, sir, if we do go down that vault.'

The architect wouldn't listen, of course. He was smiling a little when he said it was a bit late for that, but when he said Withers could stay up top, Withers' sense of honour made him say, 'Oh no, sir, I must go too.'

Jewson went down the steps, his torch beaming into the darkness. What could Withers do but follow? Soon he stood breathing the dank, fetid air of the vault; air only used by the dead, and tasting of it. He tried not to look at the lead coffins lining the walls which the others were flashing their torches at. There was Lady Juliana's coat of arms with – he shuddered – a skull pictured above it, and crumpled in the corner was a heap of old coffin bits … and bones. Though it was hot down there he felt a sudden chill – as if a cold hand had touched his brow.

All four left as fast as they could, the others laughing and making light of it, pleased there was no subsidence. Withers shook his head and looked at his companions – three of them in their fifties at best and that Jewson ten years younger. Which one of them would it be?

The next day he found out. Lord Gainsborough's agent was taken ill. Within two days he was dead. Withers blamed himself. He should have spoken up sooner; he shouldn't have let them do it. When the folks who lived in the gatehouse told him Lady Juliana was walking again, he was not surprised. That chill he'd felt in the vault must have been her spirit slipping out of the vault to walk out whatever memories tormented her.

The vault is long closed up, and in time Lady Juliana's spirit did quieten. But what will happen if the vault needs to be opened again? Will Lady Juliana walk once more? Will someone else have to die?

5

THE PRIOR'S GUEST

The Prior saw how tired his brethren were at matins that morning. They had struggled all yesterday to make repairs to the bridge. There were only five of them. As he stepped out of the little chapel the Prior blinked in the sunshine of this new summer's day. Such a morning should fill one with hope and possibility, but the priest had grown weary in his office. His humble priory, the Hospital of St John the Baptist, had no money and too few brothers. The buildings, the mill, the gardens, the bridge were slowly falling apart and he was powerless to prevent it. Some said the hospital should be closed down. What then would become of the poor and sick who came here in need? What would become of the bridge over the Thames, which the hospital was charged to maintain?

The Prior eyed the bridge across the river's glistening expanse, and its sagging central pier that had never been right since the Duke of Gloucester had wrecked the bridge during his rebellion against Richard II. He saw a dark-cloaked man crossing over the bridge from the Berkshire side. He might have been heading to Lechlade or beyond, but the Prior's instinct was paid off by a sinking feeling of inevitability as the man, moving with an unsteady gait, lurched off the highway to the hospital gate.

He was a man long past youth, with hair and beard grown long and filthy and salted with grey. His eyes stared wide and swivelled in different directions as he spoke. The Prior felt a shiver up his spine. He was well acquainted with afflictions of the soul and he guessed at once that this man was a man possessed. With a silent prayer to the Lord for strength, the Prior led the stranger to the guesthouse and poured him some ale.

The man drank greedily, for he had walked far; and then he made his confession to the Prior's patient ear.

'You might call me a natural philosopher. It was my calling, I believed, to investigate the mysteries of creation: the properties and the functions of minerals, potions, vegetables, beasts. I travelled far, into Flanders, Germany, Italy, and talked with great thinkers of our time. I invested all my wealth in a house in which I built a workshop to carry out my experiments. Most of all, I pursued the greatest mystery of creation: the means of life and death of the human form.'

The Prior stirred in his chair. 'Does not that mystery lie in the purview of Our Lord's promise of resurrection in the life hereafter?'

One of the man's eyes stared at the priest while the other flicked around the spartan room and its simple images of Christ on the cross, the Virgin and Child, and St John the Baptist. 'Such things', he replied, 'belong to a realm beyond the created world that can be apprehended by our senses and reason. What I desired to understand was the secret that sustains life in the body as we know it in this present world. Some have sought this secret in the quest for the philosopher's stone. I say you might as well chase the rainbow's end. Instead I examined piece by piece the structure and mechanism of the body itself – the bones, organs, muscles, the veins, nerves, guts, and gristle. Many were the corpses I purchased or stole. But it was not enough to merely examine. To test my theories of how life is sustained, to discover how life could triumph over death within this mortal world, I had to be creative too. I had to bring life into being from death.'

Again the Prior stirred uneasily. 'Surely the creation of life is the prerogative of God alone?'

'You, of course, would say so, Father, and perhaps I have learnt to my cost it were better so.' For an instant both the man's eyes focused together upon the Prior, before each jerked away in a different direction. His body trembled. His hands involuntarily clawed at the air. 'It was a temptation of power. Once I possessed the knowledge, once I had in my hands the power to accomplish something no man had done before, I spared no thought for the whys and wherefores. There seemed no choice but to do what lay within reach. To do it because I could.'

'Yet you *did* have a choice, did you not?'

'There was a moment when I said to myself, "Shall I do this thing?" After all the years of toil that had brought me to that point the answer could only be yea. And so I made it – or rather "her". The form of a woman as beautiful as any sculpted by Praxiteles. If she was to be immortal, I reasoned, she should be perfect in every way. Parts of the bodies of a score of women went into her, as every component had to be uncorrupted by disease or decay or natural imperfection. I used clay also, and crystals, and salt potions, to enable her body to endure while others succumbed to the ravages of time.

'Thus I made her and she lay white and beautiful on my work-shop bench. Yet she had not life. That I had to ignite in her with my own living breath. As God breathed life into Adam, so I breathed life between the pale lips of my creature. Again and again I gave her this kiss of life, till at last her fair bosom began to rise and fall and her strong heart began to beat. Then she opened her eyes and in her crystal gaze the passion of twenty Helens stared up at me …'

Here the alchemist's words faltered. The Prior was listening with bated breath. 'I am a priest of Our Lord and this is your confession. Speak on.'

'The truth is that I did more than breathe life into her. I lay with her as a man lies with a woman. She demanded it as if it were a requirement of her coming to life. I lay with her all the night and felt my soul invaded by something vast and other, whose power overwhelmed me so that I felt almost a stranger in my own body. Dawn broke, and in the sunlight shining through the window her crystal gaze seemed a demon's. She had the appetite of twenty women, a power over me I could not resist. I became like a beast in the form of a man. I hardly knew who I was. For six days I did not leave that house. In those six days so greatly did she tax me that my flesh shrivelled on my bones.'

The Prior was on the edge of his seat, eyes goggling. 'And on the seventh day … ?'

'On the seventh day, I remembered – in that small part of my mind I yet possessed – how God had rested after the six days of his labour. I muttered the Lord's Prayer, mindlessly, like a charm, and somehow I found the strength to flee from her. I felt a wrenching of pain, like tearing off my own limb, or severing the bond of flesh between conjoined twins. She screamed like an army of devils. She pleaded with her crystal gaze. When I slammed the door behind me I heard a gasping sigh like steam releasing from a pot. I looked through the window and she was standing quite still, white as quartzite, a graven image perfect and beautiful.

'I abandoned everything: house, workshop, books, apparatus. I left it all and ran. But I did not find peace. Though I escaped from the thing I had created, I could not escape the memory of what had happened.' The man's face was a grimace of torment. His eyes darted this way and that. His fingers grasped at the air. His body jerked and twitched. 'I still hear the voices screaming inside me. They never cease. I have hardly slept in all these years.

Often I've thought of ending my life; but I dare not do that for terror of what will happen to my soul. I have wandered like a tramp, scavenging food and shelter where I can. Then, not seven days ago, I shared a crust with another wayfarer on the banks of this great river and, in crude blessing of the food, he chanced to speak the name of John the Baptist.

'I said to him, "Why did you call upon that saint?"

'"Dunno," he said, "unless tis on account of the 'ospital of the aforementioned, up the river by Lechlade. A body can scrounge a fair meal up there."

'I had an impulse then that was not of my own will, or of the voices that torment me, but a bidding that seemed to come from beyond. I will not call it "hope", as I have long abandoned that sentiment.'

The Prior marvelled at the story he had heard. Amidst all its horrors he discerned the hand of God.

'You acted upon that bidding,' he said. 'And now you have made your confession. Know that God yet loves you and has not forsaken you. Will you come with me to the altar of Our Lord and receive absolution?'

The hospital's little chapel was not the place for what had to be done. It was too intimate a part of the brothers' home. Instead the Prior led his wild-eyed guest by the long straight path through the hospital precinct to the parish church of St Mary in Lechlade. There the man knelt before Christ crucified and the Virgin's loving gaze. The Prior put on his surplice, swung the censer to make a cloud of incense, sprinkled holy water on the penitent's matted hair, and signed the cross in the air. Then he took a deep breath and began the rite of exorcism.

As the prayers were repeated and again repeated, the man's face and limbs vibrated as if from a seething pressure within. The violence of his shaking intensified till it looked as though his body might explode. Then a high-pitched wail burst from his lips, for all the world like a woman's cry, and in the cloud of incense above him appeared the fleeting shape of a woman. A second time the man violently trembled, and there came a second cry, a woman's again but with a different intonation, and again the ghostly outline of a woman, this one smaller and slenderer, flickered through the incense. Then a third cry, and a third woman, different again, flashed into the beyond. So it went on. There were a score of them in all.

By the time the last one, with a thin shriek, passed out of him and out of this world, he was lying on the stone floor, almost unconscious. The Prior took the man's weight on his shoulder as he helped him stagger back to the hospital. There he slept non-stop for two whole nights and a day.

When he woke on the third day, the summer sun was shining bright through the window. The Prior, sitting beside the bed, saw the change in him as soon as his eyes blinked at the light and then focused steadily upon the priest. His lined features had softened. He was at peace at last. Pray God the souls of all those women had found peace too where they had gone. Weary though he was, the Prior felt a tide of gladness to be head of this hospital. It might be run-down and in penury, but it served a purpose.

More than one purpose, in fact.

He said to his guest, 'You being a natural philosopher, do you know anything about repairing bridges?'

The man eased himself up in his bed. 'I'm not as strong of limb as I once was, if it comes to lifting stone and timber, but I am well versed in the arts of mechanics and materials. I can help you fix that bridge.' And he looked through the window to the sunlit world outside.

41

6

THE PHANTOM NARROWBOAT

It was a moonless night, the best time to commit a murder, and Todd Blewitt was leaving nothing to chance. If anyone had seen him and his partner Jos Davis come rolling out of the Beauchamp Arms in Dymock that night, holding each other up as Jos sang mournful songs all the way back to their narrowboat, they would have assumed they were the best of friends.

So they had been, once. They'd had some fine times together, right back to when they were bitty lads and Jos's dad told them tales of hauling up the bones of elephants and hippos from the cut of the new canal when they were making the tunnel at Oxenhall. In the late 1840s, when the canal finally ran all the way from Hereford to Gloucester, they clubbed their money together to buy a narrowboat to haul coal. At first they thought their own Newent coal beds would make their fortune. Like everyone else, they found there simply wasn't enough coal.

Nowadays they plied their trade from Hereford to Gloucester and back again, but it was clear that that was never going to make their fortune either. Todd had a family to feed and a lad who would do on the boat now his legs were long enough to leg the tunnels. The canal would never make enough for two families, but it would make a good living for one.

Back on the boat, Todd produced a bottle of gin and a couple of cups. Jos drank his down eagerly enough. Since his wife had died he'd been hitting the bottle more. Todd just watched. Jos was so drunk and miserable these days, it would be a kindness what he was about to do.

Jos soon fell into drunken sleep. When Todd was sure his partner wouldn't wake, he crept out, as quiet as you like, and put the horse in her harness. The narrowboat moved silently off down the canal towards Newent.

They soon came to the entrance to the tunnel. Daisy knew what to do and stopped to wait for the lad to lead her over the top. But in the darkness no one was there. Todd tied her up and reassured her he'd be back, then he squared his shoulders and returned to the boat.

Jos stayed slumbering as Todd got into position for the legging. His legs felt like jelly already at the thought of what he was going to do, and he'd not yet legged an inch. It was some undertaking, he knew, to leg the Oxenhall Tunnel all by himself, but now he was set on his course he couldn't turn back. He had to think of his family. Usually, he and Jos legged together, one on either side of the boat. Tonight Todd positioned himself on the top of the boat and reached his legs up to the ceiling.

It was a far harder job than with two, and keeping the boat straight without a buddy to help was the devil, but he did it. His legs were wobbling by the time they had reached the middle of the tunnel. He hauled himself down from the roof and waited for the boat to drift to a stop. Jos was still out for the count, so Todd began the next part of the plan. He'd filched some of Daisy's straw, which he now gently eased into Jos's lolling mouth until it was stuffed full.

Then he tipped him into the canal.

Quick as a flash, before he could think about what he'd done, change his mind, haul out his friend, he was back on the top again, legging as fast as he could. He could already hear thrashing in the water, the walls echoed with coughs, moans, and desperate splashing, but he legged on. He'd made his choice.

Jos's cries followed him until he was nearly out of the tunnel. Once clear, he moored up on shaky legs and shed a few bitter tears, but the deed was done and there was no use crying over spilt milk.

He gave out the story that he'd bought Jos out and Jos had gone to London to seek his fortune there. Understandable that he'd wanted to get away, he said, what with his wife dying and no children to comfort him.

Then the body was found in the tunnel and it was obvious that it was Jos. Todd ended his life hanging from a scaffold. As he died he heard Jos's moans over and again and saw himself standing by the tiller on that dark night, all alone save for the plodding of the old horse as he made his way up to House Lock.

The Hereford and Gloucester Canal was doomed as well. It had never had enough water and there wasn't enough coal. It was bought by the Great Western Railway and part of it converted into a railway. The tunnel remained, though, still and silent and losing water every day till now there's hardly anything but mud in there.

The stretch of canal from the restored lock at Oxenhall up to Cold Harbour Bridge has become a lovely place to walk on a sunny day. But at night it is quite different.

Jamie and Vicky had parked their car by the bridge and walked out to Newent that evening. It was late when they made their way back, the moon high in the sky and shining on the canal and the pound.

'And they say,' said Jamie as they walked towards the bridge, 'that there's the ghost of a hippo in the tunnel. You can hear it go "hurrugh" even from the bridge!'

Vicky laughed. 'You're pulling my leg!'

'Well, maybe I am,' said Jamie. 'There's no hippo in there now. I heard about it from this loony storyteller guy down the George. But the navvies did find ancient hippo and elephant bones when they first dug out the canal.'

Vicky had stopped listening. The moonlight was magical, glinting on the weed-clogged water and illuminating the skeletal trees about to burst into spring leaf. Somewhere on the pound a moorhen trilled. But as Vicky looked towards the bridge she saw something strange. Something she didn't remember from their walk down.

'Jamie, there's no way you'd get a boat on the canal now, is there?'
'Of course not,' he laughed. 'You saw how shallow it was. Why?'
'Because there's one coming towards us right now.'

Jamie looked up incredulously, but Vicky was right; a long,
dark thing was coming towards them along the canal. It looked
for all the world like a narrowboat. It was a black shape on the
water, but the moonlight kept glinting on the surface as the boat
came nearer. Vicky grabbed Jamie's hand. The boat wasn't in the
water at all; it floated just above the water and the weed, and it
was so silent. Then Vicky gasped as she saw the rope that floated
tautly ahead of it as if there should be a horse pulling – and in
the moonlight she glimpsed, for just a moment, the shadowy
lines of the animal.

They stayed rooted to the spot as the boat drew level. A working
narrowboat with dark cloth covers and the cabin hidden at the
back. If it weren't for the fact it didn't touch the water, it would
have seemed so real. It was so dark and silent, but as it passed they
realised they could see right through it to the trees on the other
side. Then they saw him. A tall dark shape standing at the tiller.
He stared ahead, as silent as the boat, and as insubstantial. A man,

45

flat-capped and waistcoated, with a set white face and hollow dark eyes staring into space.

Jamie and Vicky clutched each other as the apparition passed by. As suddenly as it had appeared, the boat was gone and they were alone by the canal again. A moorhen called once more and they nearly shot out of their skins. It was a quick and anxious walk up to the car, but they saw nothing more that night. Only later did they find out about the murder and realise what they'd seen.

7

TOBY

There was a man who lived with his wife and four sons in a red sandstone cottage at the top of a hill near Longhope. He had a dog called Toby who was very loyal to him. Every day the man would cycle home from work, but the lane up to the cottage was so steep that he had to get off and push. Every day, at half past five, Toby would trot down to the last bend in the lane and wait for him at the foot of a big plum tree, a tree so old it produced little fruit any more. Before the last push up the lane the man would sit for a rest beside the dog and the two of them would gaze companionably across the valley to May Hill and Huntley Hill. From time to time Toby glanced sidelong at the man with a proud, contented air.

In the spring the hedgerows lit up with the colours of celandines and dandelions, alkanet and bluebells, lady's smock and garlic mustard, violets and herb Robert. The lane was like a pathway up to paradise. But the man was not as young as he used to be and in hot sunshine it was hard work pushing his bike up that hill. On hot summer days his younger sons would run down with bottles of cool lemonade or ginger beer and wait with Toby till their father appeared. Sometimes they were a bit late and he'd already be there, sitting in silent fellowship with his dog. But one exceptionally hot day they found the bicycle dumped in the middle of the lane and their father supine on the ground, unable to get up, and Toby anxiously licking his face as if he thought that might help.

'My chest … it hurts …'

The youngest boy, Jack, sprinted home to fetch the two eldest brothers, strapping big lads who managed to carry their dad up the steep track to the house. Their mother rushed in from the garden to call the doctor. It was no good. Before the doctor got there the man's heart had stopped.

In the sad days after, Toby remained a creature of habit. At half past five he would slip away from the cottage. He'd be away for hours till someone noticed he hadn't come for his dinner. Then young Jack would go to find him. Jack knew where to go. Down the lane to the plum tree and there would be Toby, in his usual place, watching and waiting for his master to come trudging up the hill. It was the same every working day, for week after week; Toby would go down to the plum tree to wait. He couldn't understand that his master was never coming home.

Then one day Toby disappeared. Jack had gone to the tree to fetch him, but the dog wasn't there. Jack called his name, walked further down the lane. The brothers and their mother searched everywhere, put the word out to neighbours and a notice in the paper. Jack went every afternoon to the plum tree. But they never found him. What exactly had happened to Toby they never found

out, presumably an accident of some kind, but they accepted in the end he must be dead.

Young Jack took it the hardest. He'd lost his father and now his father's beloved dog was gone as well. He lost concentration at school. He moped about instead of playing. He sat alone by the plum tree for hours.

It was nearly a year after Toby disappeared that, late one afternoon, Jack came racing breathlessly into the cottage. 'I've seen Toby! Down by the tree!'

His brothers rushed down the lane to see. When they got to the old plum tree, no dog was to be seen. For a while they called his name, half-heartedly, since it was plain to the three elder brothers that Toby had not been there. Jack had made it all up because he wanted Toby back so much.

They could forgive him that once. But the next day the same thing happened: when Jack got home from school he said he'd seen Toby again. His brothers just groaned. So this time his mother went with him to look. Just in case. But there was no sign of the dog.

'O Jacky, I know you miss Toby, but you have to accept he's gone.'

'You don't believe me, do you?' – and Jack burst into tears.

That wasn't the end of it. Every weekday Jack would be late home from school and claim he'd been sitting under the plum tree with Toby like his father used to do. His brothers grew more and more annoyed. They too missed Toby, and they missed their dad. It was like a bad joke that Jack tediously insisted on repeating. When they told him so, he would cry.

'I'm not making it up!' he bawled. 'I see him. He's really there.'

Their mother got upset too. She was still grieving more than anyone, though she tried to hide it from the boys, and she was distressed by the ill feeling Jack's stubborn claims had stirred up in the house. The eldest son was even threatening to move out.

So she decided to take action. In good time before Jack left school, she slipped down the lane and hid in the ragged hedge of willow and ivy near the old plum tree. By force of surprise she was going to make Jack admit that Toby wasn't there.

It was a warm summer's day again. She'd been sitting there a while, dozy in the sun, admiring the view across the valley and thinking about picking some flowers for the table, when she saw Toby.

He was lying stretched out low with his head resting on his paws as he kept watch down the lane where he might have expected her husband – or Jack – to come. His mottled colouration blended with the earth and dead leaves at the foot of the plum tree.

'Toby?' she whispered.

The dog just carried on staring down the lane. She crept forward and very tentatively, hand trembling, reached out to stroke him. Just before her fingers touched his fur he disappeared. She sat there, heart pounding, not knowing what to think, till Jack came trudging up the lane. He glanced automatically at the spot where Toby had been. Then he saw his mother. She flung out her arms and hugged him very tight.

'You've seen him?' Jack said.

'I'm so sorry we didn't believe you' – and she hugged him again.

They sat down together under the tree and she listened as Jack told her about Toby.

'He never reacts when you talk to him; it's like he doesn't know you're there. If you try to touch him he disappears. And he doesn't stay long. He's usually here if you come at the right time, but after a while he sort of fades away.'

None of the other brothers ever saw Toby. They didn't want to; they'd moved on. Their mother did see him a few more times and she persuaded the brothers to accept that Jack saw what he saw and maybe needed to see. Jack continued to stop under the old plum tree and sit awhile with Toby; but not every day now. As the years went by he saw him less and less often.

And with the passing years the plum tree produced less and less fruit. That was the reason the farmer who owned the land decided to cut down the old tree. It wasn't doing any harm. It wasn't dead. It had been part of that lane since before anyone could remember. But one winter day when Jack came up the lane he found only a stump and a great pile of logs, stacked to be taken away as firewood.

The place changed after that. It was hard to picture Toby sitting beside that stump. Weeds soon flourished in the light-filled gap. The stump became overgrown with ivy, and in time new trees grew along the lane and blocked the view from that spot. After the plum tree came down, Toby was never seen again.

8

MOLLY THE DREAMER

It was the end of a long day of walking for the two hikers.

'Only a mile or so to Minchinhampton,' said Jeff, consulting the map as they emerged from Hampton Fields.

'It's going to be good to get these boots off,' smiled Dave.

'But there's a couple of things marked here …'

Dave dutifully leaned over the map, squinting a little because the light was fading. '"Woefuldane Bottom"! That's great! And the "Long Stone" and a long barrow. Let's go and have a look.'

Through a gateway they found the barrow, Gatcombe Tump, a low mound grown over with beech trees that shuddered in the soft spring breeze.

'Look, you can see the stones where the entrance was,' said Dave. 'I'm going in.'

There was an electric fence around the mound, but the two walkers ducked under it with no trouble and shoved through the brambles to the stones. Then, from nowhere, they heard a siren. A Land Rover screeched to a halt. Two policemen leapt out and ran towards them.

'Stop!' one of them cried. 'What do you think you're doing?'

The full security check took a long time. It was dark by the time the police gave them leave to go.

'How dare they?' Dave fumed. 'Just because Princess Anne lives at the end of that drive!'

'And now we have to walk to the town in the dark,' muttered Jeff. 'Don't think we'll bother with the Long Stone.'

Snapping on their headtorches, they stamped off down the road. After a while, their anger cooling, they slowed down and turned off the torches so as to appreciate being out in the night. There was a sliver of a moon, and the country was quite open, but they both immediately found the dark oppressive. They felt the backs of their necks prickle. There was no sound, nothing tangible, just a sense they were not alone. They glanced at each other and were both relieved – and a little worried – to find the other affected in the same way.

'It's probably the police, making sure we're heading to Minchinhampton,' whispered Dave. He took a deep breath and looked round.

At Dave's gasp, Jeff turned as well. On the road behind them, near the gate to the barrow, was a figure. It was a man's height, dark against the starry sky. And it was moving towards them. Not walking, exactly, but coming smoothly this way, flowing, rippling in and out of vision, almost gliding, getting closer by the moment.

'Shit!' cried Jeff.

The two of them exchanged a glance then broke into a run.

The owner of the B&B noticed that the two men were out of breath and nervous when they arrived. He asked what was wrong. Nodded sagely when they explained about the dark figure.

'So you saw one on them Danes as fought the Romans, did you? They do say there was a battle there, long ago, and those mounds hold the dead warriors. Load of nonsense, I say, but there was one, Molly the Dreamer, back in my grandmother's grandmother's time, who did say as she'd spoken to them.'

Molly was walking, walking fast, as if someone was following her. When she looked around she saw she was at Woeful Dane's Bottom and a mist was rising around her. From the mist came a figure with long golden hair and dressed in a richly embroidered tunic and a fur cloak.

'Molly Dreamer,' he said, and his voice seemed to come from far away, wispy and distant, so she had to strain to hear it. 'I am Wolfhang that fought and died here nigh on a thousand years ago. I have come from beyond the grave to tell thee of the treasure buried in my mound.'

The mist parted to reveal Gatcombe Tump.

Molly stood stock still. 'Treasure?' she said. 'And how do I get it?'

Wolfhang smiled, and leaned in so close that she could smell his earthy breath as he whispered in her ear.

Molly sat bolt upright in bed and blinked into the darkness. She shook her snoring husband awake and hissed in his ear, 'Husband, I've a-dreamed – and we'm to be rich!'

Everyone trusted Molly's dreams, including Molly and her man, so the very next night they were ready with shovels, a bag for the swag, and the ghost's instructions safe in Molly's head. They tiptoed through the town and then went faster once they got to the common fields. In the moonlight they could see the Long Stone like a beacon to guide them.

'We'll be gone by midnight, now, won't we, woman? I got no wish to see that thing run round the field as they say he do,' said Molly's man with a nod to the stone.

Molly just smiled and said, 'The Long Stone won't trouble us even if he do run down to the stream. Tis the black dog as we must ware. He bent no friend to no one, and not likely to be, being as he ain't no yud.'

Her husband swallowed, and looked around, sure there was something in every shadow, but he didn't dare say anything, as Molly was an unstoppable force once she got started.

They soon reached the tump and clambered up among the brambles and young beech saplings. Molly squinted this way and that, then she marched to the head of the mound that was nearer the road. 'Now this be what we'll do. We dig till us hit his pot of gold. Then, with our hands on it, I must say a form of words.' She hesitated, then went on, 'I do hope I gets them right. He didn't half speak quiet-like.'

Their shovels bit into the moist earth and they dug away. Up came the brambles, roots and all, then piles and piles of earth, and then – chink!

Molly leant down, and with her hands firmly on the pot she cried, 'Come up! Labour in vain!'

A wind ripped through the trees, the young leaves quaked, and from nowhere and everywhere came a moaning, not the wind, but a human noise, sounding lost and far far away – and there, rising up, chilling them as it did, was a misty form that swirled and whirled and then hung above them. Wolfhang! But how different he was! Grey-skinned, hollow-eyed, with a corpse's grin and blood flowing from a dozen wounds and more. He reached out his hand, claw-like, with cracked and withered skin still clinging to the bone.

Molly and her man didn't wait for it to reach them. They turned tail and they ran. But as they raced away into the big field Molly's husband realised with a new rush of horror that something was missing. The Long Stone was gone, a gaping hole in its place. Far off, he heard the bells of Minchinhampton Church, and then, right behind him, he heard a terrible grinding sound, like stone striking stone. When he looked, there was the Long Stone curflummoxing arse over tip across the field towards him. He gave a cry and raced off faster than he'd done since he was a boy.

They got no sleep that night. At dawn Molly dragged her husband back to Woeful Dane's Bottom to retrieve their shovels and sack. In the clear morning light, dew sparkling on the grass and brightening the fresh green beech leaves, all looked innocent up there. The Long Stone stood in its place with not a blade of grass flattened around it. When they arrived at the tump the hole they'd dug had gone and the earth and grass and brambles were just as they were before.

The next night, Molly dreamt again. A dream of war and blood and horror. She was once again at Woeful Dane's Bottom, but now swords were flashing and clashing around her, men battling up and down the valley. She saw Wolfhang fighting with a black dog by his side, then saw the man fall, his enemies pounce on him with their swords, the dog barking and biting until a sword clipped off his head, and blood was lapping against her feet, rising higher and higher, rising above her ankles …

She didn't breathe a word of *that* dream to her husband, but the following night – long after midnight – the two of them set out once more with their shovels and bag to Gatcombe Tump. The digging was easier this time. They soon reached the pot.

'Come up! Labour in vain!' cried Molly, and they braced themselves.

Up rose the spectre, all open wounds and staring eyes. Molly caught a movement beside her and grabbed her husband's coat to stop him from bolting.

'Well done, Molly Dreamer,' groaned the ghost. 'The gold is waiting … but first thy man must prove his worth.' He spun to face Molly's cowering husband. 'Name thee me five parish churches.'

Molly sat back, surprised. Had she truly expected something for nothing? A quick glance at her husband made her heart sink. He was staring goggle-eyed at the ghost, his mouth open.

'Let me do it,' said Molly.

The apparition shook his head. 'The man is the master of the house. It must be him.'

Molly went bright red at that indignity, then joggled her husband's arm. 'Come on, thee great gapesnatch! Five parish churches – it yent hard!'

The poor man tried to gather his wits. All thought of churches seemed distant. Think! Come Sunday where would he be?

'Well,' he began, 'there be our Holy Trinity at Minch, and there be Holy Cross down Avening way, and …' He frowned, then inspiration struck. 'That's easy, that is, that new church in Amberley, that be Holy Trinity too.' With that the inspiration died and he stuttered to a halt.

'That's three!' cried Molly. 'Come on, thee neddy, don't give up!'

'Molly Dreamer,' intoned the spectre, 'thou must let him speak alone.'

The husband thought hard, but he'd never been much of a man for the church. He was married to Molly, wasn't he, with her potions and dreams? He remembered one time he'd been down to Stroud – but could he remember the saint's name? Suddenly another came: 'Christ Church in Chalford!'

A long silence followed. Then a long, low howl from out in the fields.

Molly's husband's jumped up in panic. 'What were that?'

As soon as he spoke the apparition began to sink.

Molly leapt up and scrabbled at the pot. '*No!* St Lawrence in Stroud – that's five! Please! Ye can't just go!'

But the earth was already piling back into the hole. Molly and her man had to jump back to escape the writhing brambles.

Molly was fuming as they set out home. But as they walked the low growl came again. From out of nowhere a dog appeared in the road in front of them, growling and snarling. They could hear it clearly, but where the sound was coming from was impossible to say because the dog had no head. Worse than that, they could see right through him to the bones. Molly recognised him at once. Wolfhang's dog was still protecting his master.

She didn't stop to tell her man. They raced on home, and when they got there he swore he was never going up there again after dark. Not for a thousand bags of gold.

Molly didn't give up so easily. She kept on digging. For years she went up to the common fields in the dead of night. When her husband died she moved out of town into a cave near the tump so she could get there more easily on her old legs. But she found nothing.

One night when Molly was an old woman she dreamt of Wolfhang again. He was as handsome as when she had first seen him, with his long golden hair and his fine clothes. He leaned down and in his hoarse, distant voice he whispered, 'Go to the Long Stone. It's waiting for you there …'

The very next evening, as soon as it was dark, Molly was out at the Long Stone with her shovel and her sack. Eagerly she dug around the stone. At first there was nothing. It began to rain. She glanced at the sky and saw the clouds roiling in, covering the moon, so it was hard to see what she was doing. She heard a rumble of thunder, but she kept on digging. The rumbles grew louder, distant flashes of light told her the storm was coming, but she was getting closer, she was sure. Her shovel hit something hard. Then came a flash of lightning and she saw, just for an instant, a stone. Thunder banged almost overhead. Slinging her shovel aside, she reached down to pull the stone up, expecting the pot to be underneath.

Lightning flashed. Her world was filled with light, there was a sharp smell of ozone and fire, then she fell to the ground.

The townsfolk found her there the next morning, sitting by the Long Stone with her hair all standing on end and a smile on her face. She was never quite the same after that. If you were to ask her about the gold, she'd simply smile and wink, and tap her pockets as if the treasure was stashed away in there.

Jeff and Dave went to bed with the story ringing in their heads. The next morning dawned bright and clear, and the owner of the B&B told them as they ate their breakfast that the Long Stone would look great in this early light if they fancied seeing it, being as they'd missed it the night before. He'd take them up there in his Land Rover, he said, if they didn't fancy the walk. Jeff looked at Dave, and Dave looked at Jeff, then as one they shook their heads. There was no way they were going to Woefuldane Bottom again.

9

LLANTHONY SECUNDA

It was lunchtime one hot summer day in Gloucester. Peter Weston and Gregory Hall had left their jackets behind in Shire Hall while they strolled down to Llanthony Priory for a smoke and some fresh air. Peter was aware of the contradiction of these two aims, but right now he was more disturbed by the perplexities of his job. On the one hand, the axing of certain social services provided by the council; on the other, the doctrine of 'choice' in the provision that was supposed to replace them; and at the same time the capping of council spending so there was no money to pay for any choices on offer.

The grounds of Llanthony Secunda Priory are a green space near the city centre, but when Peter and Gregory got there they realised

why they didn't go there more often. Piles of building waste languished amidst the weeds and dog muck. The medieval ruins were crumbling into rubble and spray-painted with graffiti. Empty oil bottles floated in the pond. In the sultry heat both men had worked up a sweat; being managers, they didn't think of taking off their ties or unbuttoning their white shirts.

'Do you know which of these buildings was what?' Peter asked.

They were aware the abandonment of the priory dated from Henry VIII's Dissolution of the Monasteries, but they knew no more than that. They eyed the half-timbered building in the centre of the site with its incongruous Victorian extension; the big roofless ruin to the north; the remains of the gatehouse and wall where they'd come in from Hempsted Lane; and to the south another roofless ruin of red brick.

'A pity Jenny isn't here,' said Gregory. 'She'd know what everything was.'

Peter was curious about that derelict brick building. The red bricks made it look oddly modern, but the windows and doorway had a churchy look that implied the building might well have been part of the priory. He wasn't a churchgoer, but he loved Gloucester Cathedral, St Michael's Tower, Greyfriars, and it seemed a shame this other bit of Gloucester's medieval heritage was being left to rot. The place seriously needed tidying up. But if the council was having to retrench its social services they certainly wouldn't have any money for that.

He picked his way through a pink sea of rosebay to the doorway of the brick building. Just weeds and fallen masonry inside, obscenities sprayed on the walls, a stink of urine. What would it have been like in there back in the day when the building was in use? He stepped through the doorway, and as he did so he felt a shiver through his body.

'Are you sure it's safe in there?' Gregory's voice behind him was strangely distant.

The brick walls didn't look imminently about to collapse. Peter took another step forwards.

Then it happened. It started with a sensation of cold, so queer on such a hot day; a shivery sensation all over his sweaty skin and up the back of his neck to the crown of his head. Then a feeling a bit like the vertigo he'd sometimes felt at the top of a sheer drop on mountains, only the sense of falling wasn't downward but kind of *inward* in the very spot where he stood. He could see all the time the red brick walls, the green weeds, the bright sunlight, but all of this was becoming distant, as if it were no longer fully present, had become a kind of memory.

He saw, right in front of him, as if huddled against the wall, a group of people. They were dressed in shapeless garments of dirty, tattered sackcloth, with hoods that shadowed their faces. Some were obviously children. The others, he knew from the way they held themselves and clung to the children, were women. Their shoulders were bowed. Their heads hung down. He'd never seen anyone, not in England, who looked quite so desperately poor, so defeated. They looked grey, insubstantial, and the brickwork of the wall was faintly discernible through their bodies.

Peter glanced to the doorway. 'Gregory, are you there?'

Yes, Gregory was standing just outside the building. When Peter turned back to where he'd been looking the women and children had gone. There was just the crumbling brick wall, the noise of traffic in the distance, and that shivery sensation on his skin, now starting to fade.

Gregory had seen nothing. Peter tried to explain what he'd seen.

'Impoverished families, eh?' said Gregory. 'These services cuts must be getting to you, making you see things.'

'No, I really saw them. Right there.' Peter pointed. Because there was patently nothing there he began to feel foolish.

The rest of that day, and the day after, he couldn't get that vision out of his mind. When he was working on the documents spelling out the council's new service provisions the sight of those hunched women and scrawny children haunted him. He felt an urge to go back to the priory, but he wanted also to understand the meaning of what he'd seen. At the end of the second day he phoned Jenny Mitchell at the Archives and asked if she'd meet him at Llanthony Priory the next day.

'Any particular reason?'

'I'd rather not say over the phone.'

'You're not planning to propose to me, are you? I am married, you know.'

When they met at the priory it wasn't quite so hot a day and Peter had kept his jacket on.

'Are you going to tell me now why I'm here?'

Jenny Mitchell was not only an archivist but also a historian. She knew a thing or two about Gloucester's past.

Peter pointed out the brick building. 'Do you know what that used to be?'

'Part of the priory. The stable, I believe.'

Peter took a deep breath and told her what he'd seen.

To his surprise, Jenny didn't smile or mock. When he said she must think the heat had got to him, she said, 'Not at all. If you take an interest in the past, old buildings especially, you do hear of strange things.'

'So … what do you think I saw? Who *were* they?'

'If somehow you've picked up a scene, an echo, from the past … well, I know that some prisoners of war were kept here awhile in the eighteenth century —'

Peter shook his head. 'I'm sure they were women and children.'

Jenny got him to describe exactly how the people in his vision were dressed.

She said, 'They do sound like landless peasants as you'd expect them to look in the Middle Ages when the priory was in use. Or maybe …'

She stopped walking and looked around at the ruined buildings – as if conjuring in her mind a picture of how the place looked back then, with its long ranges of accommodation enclosing a grassy quadrangle where they now stood, and further back, where the ship canal today cuts through, the priory church and cloister.

'In those days,' she continued, 'paupers who had no food, no home, nowhere else to go, would come to the monasteries. It was the nearest thing to a welfare system. When the breadwinner of a family died, his widow could be destitute, with no means to earn a living and provide for her children. Such women might band together for safety on the road and make their way to a monastery where the monks would give them food and maybe space in the stables where they could stay for a time.'

'So people like that could have come here?' said Peter.

'Certainly. The priory was pretty wealthy; it could afford to be charitable.'

'But the women I saw looked so terribly defeated.'

'That's what I was thinking about.' Jenny gestured at the derelict ruins. 'When the monasteries were dissolved, that flimsy welfare system was taken away. Llanthony Priory was surrendered to the Crown in 1539. Its whole estate was sold for a song to one of the King's cronies, the Gloucester MP Arthur Porter, who had no interest in the house except as a source of building stone. In just a few years the place was a ruin.'

In silence they proceeded to the ruined brick stable. Peter wanted to go in, to see if the vision would reappear, but when he remembered that feeling of falling through time he hesitated. He steeled his nerves, lifted his foot, began to step through the empty doorway — But some force in the air blocked his way like an invisible locked door that he'd walked right into. He felt once again that chill shiver all over his skin and up the back of his neck, the prickling of his hair standing on end. And he felt something else – a heart-wrenching pang of dismay, as if all hope had been torn away. He thought of those poor women, pictured them trudging with their hungry children to this place that had once given them succour, only to find the priory empty, its buildings derelict, its doors locked.

Peter Weston was very thoughtful as he walked back to Shire Hall that afternoon and contemplated the work waiting on his desk. Rolling out the cuts in social services. What could he do, someone like him, whose job was to implement policy and not ask why, in a time when a new broom was sweeping away the safety net on which the most vulnerable depended? Had he been shown that vision for a reason?

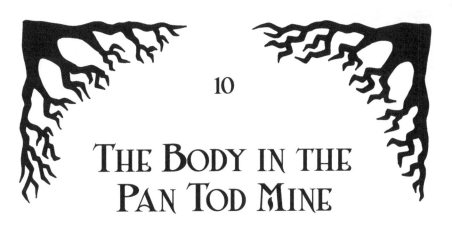

10

THE BODY IN THE PAN TOD MINE

The top of Ruardean Hill was packed with people that summer's day in 1844. More than a hundred men, women, and children jostled to get close to the head of the old Pan Tod Mine, where the horses in the horse wheel patiently stood. One of the constables was blowing his whistle and shouting, 'Get back, get back!' as people pressed too close to the open shaft and the waiting coffin.

Timothy Mountjoy, twenty years old, a miner at the Duck Pit near Cinderford and a strict Baptist, was straining forward with the best of them. It seemed half the Forest had turned out, and there was a festival atmosphere. Timothy didn't approve. He was here to witness, but this was a serious event. There should be no joy in seeing a body, especially if it had been in the mine four years and more.

The local constables and a team from the True Blue Colliery at Ruardean had gone down on a chain link. The six of them had perched on the loops of chain as they were lowered, Davy lamps clutched in their hands. The constables, who'd been down before, had looked full of fear. Whatever was now going on down there, hidden from view, those above could only wait.

The reason they were all there was that the one trapped down there couldn't wait. Not any more. After four long years the thing in the pit was ready to come out, and was making sure everyone knew it.

'Is it Get-it-to-go down there, like they say?' Timothy asked the man next to him, whom he vaguely knew, a miner at True Blue.

The man went white and turned away, twisting his cap in his hand.

The woman the other side of Timothy shot the True Blue miner an evil glare. 'He was a Pan Tod miner before,' she muttered to Timothy. 'Got things on his mind, I reckon.'

Timothy stared at her, not taking in for a moment what she'd implied. Then understanding dawned. Did she mean this man had had a hand in Get-it-to-go's demise?

The mine had been shut those four years since the stonecutter they called Get-it-to-go had disappeared from Ruardean Hill. The owner, some foreigner, had also not been seen in the Forest again. But it wasn't long after it closed that rumours had drifted as far as Littledean Hill, where Timothy lived, that the pit wasn't as empty as it should be. That there was a dead man down there and he was not resting easy.

Ghosts! In Littledean they were familiar with ghosts. Wasn't the Hall infested with them, black boys and Cavaliers and monks, and hadn't his own sister seen the Grey Lady, Lady Betty, under the old chestnut, the moot tree by the Hall? But Timothy had been sceptical. The only time he thought he'd seen a ghost, it had turned out to be a calf and its dam.

This was the third time the constables had gone down the pit. Each previous time they'd come back with nothing. No bones, no sighting, nothing. There was just that awful knocking sound the family in the cabin next to the pit complained about. The first time, they'd just lowered a couple of men down using a windlass, since all the gear was gone from the shaft head. The second time, the knocking having got louder and more frequent, they'd re-erected the horse wheel.

After that, Timothy and his friends decided to go up to Ruardean Hill one night and read their Bibles by the mine, to see if scripture would calm the spirit – if there was a restless spirit at all.

When they got up there, the wife of the little house by the pit – no more than a cabin – came out and told them the tale. 'That stonecutter, Get-it-to-go, he was a fine man, able to fix any of them machines as you miners like to use. Maybe he missed his calling. Maybe that's what drove him to the liquor so often. Not like you God-fearing boys. They say as that last night he was at a place where drink is sold.' The woman frowned, and, before it was barely begun, her story was over. 'Well, walking home, he fell down the mine. Now he's clamouring to get out.'

The young men weren't convinced by her tale. They took themselves over to the old mine, threading their way carefully through the old workings, the dips and ruts of the cart tracks.

'I heard there was a quarrel,' said one lad. 'Up here, after hours, and he took, you know, an unlucky blow, and that's what sent him down there.'

The hill was still and silent. In the moonlight they could see a further line of hills across the dark valley. The mineshaft was all boarded up, courtesy of the constables' last visit below.

'Nobody found anything,' began Timothy. 'But —'

From beneath them, and all around, there came a knocking and a banging, as if someone was using a hammer and drill right down below them in the pit, just as if the pit was still active. It went on and on. A baby started wailing in the cabin. The boys sat there with their Bibles tight in their hands, not daring to move.

Then one lad said, in a small wavering voice, 'My grandda do say there are them as live in the mines. Little tiny colliers, he says, with shining eyes —'

'Hush now!' hissed Timothy. 'Where's your faith? There are no little folk – and that ghost down there, if that's what it is, wants a blessing from God!'

In that moment, it seemed, the banging got louder. The door of the cabin burst open and out shot the woman. 'Go on now! Get! You've only made him angry!'

That night, tossing and turning in his bed, Timothy had one of those strange true dreams he sometimes got. He saw, as if a long way off, an argument on Ruardean Hill, men swearing awful oaths, a voice with a different accent calling out in fear, and then a body falling, falling. He was shivering when he woke. He prayed then, hoping he'd seen the past, not the future like when he'd dreamt Tom Wintle was crushed by a falling beam and that very day Jeb Annis was caught under rubble in the mine and died.

The following day he heard they were going to send the constables down again. He took it as a sign, and off he went to Ruardean.

Timothy drew his coat closer round his neck and stared across the gorse and heather spreading over the old workings, thinking about the consciences – and the souls – of those who had done the deed.

After six years in the mines he could easily imagine what it was like for the men down there. Down in the pit it was a hell of heat and stink. Damp earth and damp coal, and something that was like that worst smell down the pit, the firedamp smell, but not quite – a sweeter smell, cloying, heavy, and foul. They'd wrapped cloth across their faces, but it didn't block the smell. The sweat pouring down their faces left streaks of pink in the black coal smears.

The constables didn't dare fail to find the body, not this time. They cleared rubble and fallen timbers as they searched, back-breaking work, with the constant nagging fear that it would all collapse and they'd be trapped like the spirit.

'Dear Christ in heaven!' cried the one who found it. Only the clothes marked that it had once been human. They were the only thing holding it together. And, oh dear God, the smell!

'Call for the coffin, quick!'

On the top the horses were moving again. The crowd watched and whispered as the coffin was lowered. They waited until at last they saw the horses start up and then – the stench that rose from the shaft! When the coffin reached the top they carried it to the green and people gathered for a look, and then there were ladies fainting, and even grown men used to the stinks of colliery or ironworks looked green and turned away to gag.

Timothy didn't go to look. That lost soul shouldn't be dishonoured by such gawking. It had been defiled enough already. As he turned away from the mine the white-faced man next to him turned too and walked away. Such a look of self-loathing on his face! Timothy knew then there was guilt in the man, that he was afraid for his soul, and his life, even if there was no nose left on the corpse for him to have to press to see if it bled and proved him a murderer.

Timothy felt an impulse to go after him, to talk to him about repentance and God's forgiveness. But it wasn't the time or the place.

That night, he dreamt again, seeing the same quarrel as before, hearing the angry shouts, then seeing the blow that pitched down the smartly dressed, spivvy-looking man, and then he was the man falling, falling, and the bottom was rushing up to meet him …

When he awoke he was puzzled. It wasn't a stonecutter he'd seen, but another man, the mine owner, the foreigner they said had gone away. And the shouting hadn't just been a drunken quarrel, but angry talk of bad pay and profits and unfairness, and when the blow had been struck and the body went down he'd seen the miners walk away.

Timothy Mountjoy never spoke of what he dreamt that night, and when he wrote about it many years later it was Get-it-to-go he mentioned, not the man he'd seen in the dream. The mine was silent by then, the spirit gone to his maker, whoever he was. But Timothy did ruminate how no man should feel that his fists were the only answer to injustice, and he strove all his life for miners' rights.

If you go up Pan Tod Beacon today, you'll see a memorial to five miners who died in mines nearby, but no mention of him who died and lay trapped in that very spot so long ago. And if you hear a knocking when you're up there … well, perhaps the spirit isn't resting as quiet as Timothy hoped it was.

11

THE ROYALIST FERRYMAN

If you glance down from the road as you drive over the Second Severn Crossing, and if the tide is out, you'll see an expanse of sandstone and weed a mile wide before the main channel of deep water. These reefs are the English Stones. When the tide is high you'll see not a prickle of them, for the tidal range here exceeds fifty feet; one of the highest in the world.

Back in the seventeenth century, during the Civil War, there was no bridge, of course. Instead there was a ferry. One evening in the middle of the war, a party of Cavaliers arrived at the little port of Redwick. They were exhausted from riding, their horses' flanks foamy with sweat, but they could not rest yet. They carried urgent dispatches from the King to his supporters in Wales. Some say Prince

Rupert himself was among them. They could not go via the bridge at Gloucester because Gloucester was held by Parliament. So to the New Passage ferry they came. And, whether by chance or by treachery, a troop of Ironsides were on their tail, only minutes behind them.

The ferry skipper understood the urgency of the moment. Like many in the west, outside the great mercantile cities of Bristol and Gloucester, his sympathies were for the King. He led the long-tressed Cavaliers and their horses down the muddy path through cordgrass to the embayment where the ferryboat waited. Horses and men were hustled aboard. It was already getting dark as the crewmen poled the twin-masted boat into the estuary. There was still a breath of wind to work into the sails. The veteran skipper steered with skill, playing his feel for wind and current against the labyrinth of reefs, a good two miles' sail, till they slid beside the jetty on the Portskewett side. Soon enough the riders were safely away to Royalist friends who would have a warm hearth and warm beds to welcome them.

The ferrymen took their time returning to the Gloucestershire side. The skipper knew well enough whom they'd find there. The wind had dropped to nothing, so they had to row, and mist was rising from the water, so he had to pick their course with great care. When they reached their mooring at Redwick the Parliamentarian troopers were waiting, their horses stamping and shivering, the milky moonlight shining from helmets and breastplates. They were a larger number than the Cavaliers, would make short work of them in a fight.

The skipper made a show of tiredness. ''Tis uncommon late, sirs. My men be lagged after a long day of graft. Ye'll find good lodgings, I warrant, at yonder inn.'

The captain of the troop placed his hand on the hilt of his sword. 'Make haste, grandad, and do your job. Put my men across.'

The ferryman gestured to the thickening fog on the river. 'It do be nation dark already, and foggy and all. Best ye wait till sun-up when there'll be breeze enough to fill the sails.'

The Roundhead captain raised the point of his sword to the ferryman's breast. 'Take us at once, you rustic scum, or it shall be the worse for you!'

The skipper didn't take kindly to being called 'scum', but there was no arguing with that shiny steel blade. Wearily he instructed his lads to guide the horses over the gangplank; too many of them really for a boat this size. The troopers clattered aboard with their mounts. Some found a place to sit; others had to stand among the horses. Still no breath of wind, so again the boatmen rowed. The long oars dipped with little splashes in the glassy stillness of the water. You could see no more than a stone's throw into the fog, thick and clammy all around them, opalescent in the moonlight. The boy in the bow peered forward through the murk. The skipper in the stern peered intensely too, feeling his way by memory and instinct, his hand steady on the tiller as the boatmen dipped their oars. The horses shifted nervously. The breath from their nostrils condensed into plumes of mist. The troopers felt in their limbs the tensions of the night – the combat they sought with the King's men, the power of the elements around them in the mouth of Britain's mightiest river.

There was a shout from the boy in the bow. The skipper called the oarsmen to ease off. One of them silently caught another's eye. As the boat drifted forwards the shore resolved from the gloom, a low line of black rock textured with the shimmer of moonlight on slimy seaweed. A few touches of the oars drew the ferry alongside it, as close as the skipper dared, and the anchor went down.

'Is there no jetty?' demanded the Roundhead captain.

'There do be one somewhere,' shrugged the ferryman, 'but this be the best as I can do in this yere fog.'

The captain gave him a cold look and eyed the gap between boat and shore. The boatmen lowered the gangplank into the water and then jumped down, waist deep in brine, to guide the skittish horses as the troopers led them down. Much splashing and scrabbling and godly restraint of curses as the Ironsides and their horses waded up the slippery shore. The captain waited till last. He handed the ferryman some coins and with a final wary glance to the shore, and back to the ferryman, he took his mare down the gangplank. One of the boatmen, a soft-eyed young fellow, gave her neck a tender stroke as she gamely struggled ashore.

The ferrymen climbed back aboard and the boat pulled away into the fog. The troopers led their steeds up the bank of rock and weed, periwinkles crunching under hooves, the fog swirling round them as a whisper of breeze began to rise. Then, to their surprise, the ground sloped downwards – and before them was open water! The captain scrambled to the water's edge, waded in a few steps, then stopped as the rocks shelved into deeper water. Through the fog he could see no end to the expanse of water, in which he discerned an oozing movement from left to right – upstream, as best he could judge it.

An oath spat from his lips as he guessed what had happened. He staggered back over the slippery crest of rock, yelling to the ferrymen. But all he could see where his troop had disembarked was smooth black water fading into the fog. In the water here too he perceived a faint movement upstream.

'God's truth!' he cried. 'They've marooned us and the tide is turning!'

Shouts to the vanished ferry erupted from the men, muffled by the fog. Cumbered by their armour and weapons, they slipped and staggered along the reef, splashing through dark unseen pools. In the downstream direction the water's edge seemed to angle back towards the Gloucestershire shore, so they followed that ragged line of black against black, hoping against hope that while the tide was low it might lead them to a gap narrow enough to wade or swim. At first they led their horses. Then they saw how the water was flowing quicker upstream, washing over rocks that moments before had stood dry. Horses were let free to take their own chances as the troopers lurched on, shouting in terror, pleading to the ferrymen, God, anyone, to come to their aid. The wind had risen. The fog began to break up. Maybe they glimpsed England's black shadow. But the space of water between was getting wider and deeper by the moment, as the Severn's flood tide spilled up the channel before them and the greater channel behind them, as the pools in the reef oozed wider, driving the men on to the highest knobbles of rock.

One desperate trooper threw off his helmet, breastplate, pistols and sword, and tried to swim. Yet faster and stronger the mighty tide came. Screams of men and horses as it overwhelmed them.

They never stood a chance, neither the men in their steel breast-plates and heavy buff coats and leather boots, nor the horses that had carried them through the adventures of war.

When the war was won, Cromwell closed down the New Passage ferry because of the Ironsides who'd drowned there. By the century's end, though, it was back in use, rivalling the Old Passage from Aust till the New Passage was finally made redundant by the railway tunnel in 1886. A century later the piers of the Second Severn Crossing were emplaced in the sturdy sandstone of the English Stones. Twice a day, as always and ever, the tide rises and falls upon those reefs, more than fifty feet each time. By day you'll hear only the roar of traffic on the M4; but go there by night when the traffic has died away, a foggy moonlit night when the tide is turning, and you may hear out there, muffled through the fog, the shouts and the screams of horses and men as the sea rushes over the rocks.

12

THE POSTHUMOUS ADVENTURES OF FRIAR JOHN

Giles Gaston stared at the body on his parlour floor and thought, 'What now?'

He and his wife Margaretta had prepared carefully for this evening. She was looking her prettiest in a fine red dress and her hair shining and loose like a maiden's. The thing is, it was her prettiness – or rather one lecherous man's reaction to it – that had got them into this pickle in the first place. He'd planned just to give their visitor a light tap on the head, but when he'd seen that oily fat monk smarming all over his lovely wife he'd seen red, the cudgel had come down with the force of anger behind it, and, well, there was the result on the floor. Friar John, the most notorious, most lecherous of all the friars at St Augustine's Abbey in Bristol lay dead and cooling on their floor.

'What are we going to do?' Giles cried.

'Well, he can't stay here.' Margaretta looked down at the body with distaste. 'O Giles, why did you do that? Wasn't the plan just to get the money and give him a scare? When I think of him leering over me in the Lady Chapel, offering me money for my charms, it makes my stomach turn – but I never wanted him dead! He'd have never dared complain to the Abbot and we'd have been well off again. And even if he just wanted to ogle me he was our friend all these long months of our poverty, bringing us food and drink when our other friends turned from us.'

Giles hung his head in shame. But in the end what's done is done. He glanced through the oriel window that looked straight out over the Frome.

'Let's heave him into the river,' he said.

Margaretta had always been more practical. 'No, Giles! He's so fat he'll pop straight up like a cork! You'd best take him back to the abbey. He'll not be missed yet. That reprobate of a monk spent every evening out in the city.'

She rummaged at the corpse's belt and discovered a bunch of long black keys.

'One of these will unlock the postern gate by the river. Just take him in there and leave him for the friars.'

They bundled the friar up in his own cloak and Margaretta helped heave the dead weight on to Giles's back.

Christmas Street was dark and deserted, thank God. As quietly as he could with such a heavy burden, Giles staggered over the bridge across the Frome and past St Bartholomew's Hospital. Then he followed the river away from the buildings and down towards the Avon. The wall of the abbey rose up before him. In the light reflected from the river he saw the little postern gate that led to the abbey fishponds. The corpse still heavy on his back, he fumbled with the keys until he found one that opened the gate. With a glance up at the abbey church on the hill, its windows glowing bright amidst the darkness, he leaned the stiffening body of the friar up against a tree and fled.

As evensong came to an end, the Abbot cast his eyes around the assembled friars and noted that – yet again – Friar John was missing.

'By the holy bones of St Augustine,' he cried, 'that sinful brother is out on the town again, bringing scandal to our brotherhood! No doubt there's a woman involved. Will anyone here go out and fetch him back?'

Henry the Almoner stepped forward. 'I'll go,' he said.

The Abbot eyed him with distrust. If John was the abbey's worst offender, then Henry was a close second. Muttering, 'Send a thief to catch a thief,' he waved Henry on his way.

Henry rubbed his hands with glee. Friar John had many friends, but Henry was not one of them, not after John's mockery of Henry's exploits – or lack of them – with the ladies. The chance to get John in trouble was too good an opportunity to miss.

He'll be out with one of his 'lady friends', thought Henry. As if they liked him! There's that Eleyn, Baldwin the miller's daughter … No, wasn't he wittering about the lovely Margaretta who lives on Christmas Street?

Henry made his way quickly down to the postern gate, but as he passed one of the fishponds he saw John standing against a tree as if meditating on the night's beauty.

'Ho John!' he called. 'What are you doing? Preaching to the fishes? Did your wench refuse you? Well, there is *someone* who wants to see you: the Abbot – and he's not best pleased.'

John just kept on staring into space, and Henry grew angry at the slight. He walked right up to John. 'Come on, you sluggard!' He gave him a shove. It was a hard, angry push and, to Henry's delight, John fell straight into the pond.

Instead of jumping up and spluttering, John just floated there. As the minutes dragged by, Henry's delight turned to fear. He jumped into the water and hauled him out, but John just lay there, cold and wet and still.

'My God, he's dead!' cried Henry. Then, in a whisper, 'I've killed him.'

He thought fast. He mustn't be found with the body. Better to pass the blame to someone in the city? Someone, say, with a comely woman in his household. Baldwin the miller was a big man in Bristol. Too risky. The Gastons, though, were too poor to pose any danger. So to John's reluctant sweetheart, Margaretta, John would have to go. Henry hauled the stiff, sopping body on to his back, and out through the postern gate he went. When he reached Christmas Street he leaned the body against the door, knocked, and ran.

When they heard the knock, Giles and Margaretta bolted up in bed, certain the authorities were after them. Margaretta nervously went down to open the door. Into her arms fell Friar John's body like a lover returning home. She shrieked in terror. Giles, when he saw, cried out, 'The Devil has brought him back to punish us!'

Margaretta let the body drop. 'Then we must trick the Devil! Everyone knows that Friar John was pursuing Eleyn, the miller's daughter, and that Dighton the butcher was after the friar's blood for trying to ruin his betrothed. So take him down to the millpond and drop him in. They'll think he was after the girl and fell in. No blame will come to anyone.'

Giles hefted the friar on to his back once again. 'Urgh, feels like he's been in the soup already! And there's me thinking that hell was hot!'

This time, instead of crossing the river, he headed down Christmas Street, through St John's Gate, and into the city. The streets were very dark. Giles's heart thumped so loud that he was sure it could be heard. As he turned into St Stephen's Street he stepped in something soft and warm and had to bite his tongue. Then it was round the bend towards Corn Street. With every step the friar's body seemed to get heavier. Once a cat yowled very near and Giles nearly dropped his burden.

At last he was at St Nicholas Steps, the mill just yards away. As he was about to turn down the steps he heard the sound of pounding feet. In the shadowy darkness he saw something coming. He slammed himself and the corpse against the wall. The friar's clammy cold cheek pressed up against his own and he had to force himself not to cry out.

At that very moment the approaching figure looked up. Giles was sure his goose was cooked, but instead the other man let out a stifled oath, dropped something large, and ran. For a long moment Giles stood there with Friar John heavy against him. When it seemed clear the man wasn't coming back, Giles left the friar propped up against the wall and went to investigate the thing that had been left behind.

It was a bag with something very large inside it. Giles struggled to open the tightly knotted ties till at last they came loose and in the dim light he saw a face staring back at him. He leapt away, swallowing his yell. He took a deep breath, peered back in, and grinned in relief. It was the face of a pig.

The question of why the man had a pig in a bag wasn't Giles's problem. He may not have been as quick as his wife, but an idea came to him that made the grin spread wide across his face.

'Exchange is no robbery,' he said, and set to work.

Meanwhile, after hiding in a doorway for some time, the pig thief crept back into the narrow alley and saw, to his relief, that the men he'd seen had gone and his bag was untouched. With a grunt he heaved it on to his shoulders and trudged on the way he'd been going. After a short distance he ducked with his burden under the lintel of an alehouse doorway.

'What's the haul tonight?' asked the waiting landlord.

The thief grinned. 'A whole hog! Filched from Dighton the butcher's.' With a flourish he pulled open the bag.

Both landlord and thief stared with horror. Friar John's bloated round face stared sightlessly back at them.

'Jesus, Mary, and all the saints!' cried the landlord. 'I know he has a reputation as a swine of a man, but I can't serve that up to tomorrow's customers!'

'But … but … it was a hog when I took it.'

They carried on staring at the dead friar till at length the landlord said, ''Tis clear to me what's happened. Everyone knows that Friar John is the biggest rakehell that abbey has. They know he chases every young skirt in the city. The Devil surely won him and turned him into a hog to punish him for his sins against that poor Eleyn, the miller's daughter – and the rest. Then Dighton must've bought the hog, killed it, and now the friar's dead and changed back into his true shape!'

'That's all very well,' cried the thief, 'but if we're caught with him, dead as he is, we'll hang!'

The landlord nodded. 'Best we put him back where you found him.'

So they bundled the corpse up again and set out through the night to the shambles by the river. They snuck into Dighton's booth, hung the friar on a hook by his habit, and fled.

Up before dawn that morning, Dighton made his way, scratching and yawning, into his booth. It was a moment or two before he saw it, but he was instantly wide awake when he did: there was

Friar John hanging limply from a hook where a pig should be, and as dead as dead could be.

'Who's played this trick on me?' he cried. 'All of Bristol heard me say I'd have his head for making calf's eyes at my Eleyn. They'll say I killed him, for certain.'

He stared at Friar John's slack grey cheeks and shivered. He knew he couldn't hesitate for long. Then it came to him. He went to his stable and led his horse quietly round to his booth. Then he tied the corpse on to the horse's back, opened the gates, gave the beast a smack on the rear, waited a moment for her to burst into the street, and then yelled, 'Stop, thief!' at the top of his voice.

People erupted from other shops in the shambles and stared as horse and rider raced past. A pair of lads made a lunge for the friar, but the horse, terrified by the smell of the dead thing on its back, was too fast. Up the High Street she went, then on to Corn Street, gaining speed down the broad thoroughfare, Friar John jouncing up and down on her back, a crowd now racing after her, yelling and shouting enough to wake the city.

Friar John listed violently as the horse galloped through St Leonard's Gate, faster and faster, heading towards the Marsh. She kept going until she saw the water's edge ahead, the great river Avon. She came to a sharp halt, and over her head sailed Friar John – to smack with an almighty splash in the river. Immediately the current swept him away. By the time Dighton retrieved his shivering horse, the body was long gone.

The whole of Bristol was alive with the gossip about how Friar John had gone mad and stolen Dighton's horse in a frenzy of jealousy over Eleyn's refusal of his advances. The only people who knew otherwise were Dighton himself, a certain thief and landlord, Henry the Almoner, and Giles and Margaretta Gaston, and none of them was saying a word.

After a week the body of Friar John was washed up at the mouth of the Avon and then transported back to his grieving brethren at St Augustine's. The Abbot decreed that, despite Friar John's misdemeanours in life, he should be accorded in death the dignity of his rank. A spot was chosen in the tranquil monks' graveyard beside the abbey church, where Friar John, in his quieter moments, had liked to take his ease with a tankard of ale. Not a year later a seedling grew up from his grave. In death Friar John nurtured a fine tree that became a landmark of the green – College Green, as it became.

That wasn't Friar John's only legacy. After the abrupt manner of his death, and his post-mortem wanderings, his spirit didn't rest easy. It is said that sometimes the figure of a monk can be seen in

Bristol Cathedral and in the Central Library next door, moving along pathways he should have frequented more often in life. Perhaps Friar John has become more pious in death. Or perhaps, since the excitements of his passing, his spirit has preferred to stay in the confines of the abbey precinct than to venture out into the city … or face up to meeting his maker.

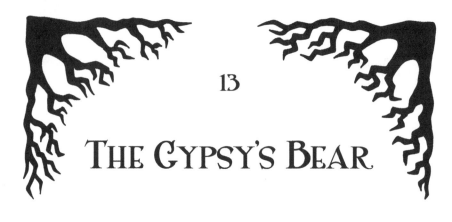

13

THE GYPSY'S BEAR

Maybe thrice a year a familiar duo would descend the road down Westington Hill to Chipping Campden. One was a swarthy-faced man, no longer young, with jet-black hair, bright ragged clothes, and on his back a strange stringed instrument shaped like a gourd. The other was a bear who shambled along leashed by a chain to his collar. They would pause at the little Conduit House, where first the man then the bear would slurp from the trough to quench their thirst. The man was a Gypsy and he'd long learnt to take his chances where he found them.

There were other Gypsy folk who passed through these parts, especially in the season of the Horse Fair at Stow, but this man and his bear never shared their company. The man was an Ursar gadular, his instrument a gadulka, and whereas the other Gypsies spoke a lively mixture of Romani and English, he was born far away in the Balkans and spoke not Romani but Romanian, a quite different tongue.

In Campden the gadular and bear would lodge in the outhouse of a thatched cottage on Heavenly Corner. They slept side by side in the straw, and twice a day the man took the bear down Blind Lane to a midden. Heavenly Corner was a peaceful spot where blackbirds sang in the trees and there was a view up Westington Hill. The bear would sometimes gaze at that green expanse of hillside as if he longed to romp there wild and free.

It was in more formidable terrain, in the pine forests of the Rhodope Mountains, that the Gypsy had found him after his mother was slain by Ottoman huntsmen. The man had cared

for the cub like his own child, fed him fruit, fish, and honey, and trained him to dance to the gadulka. Many years had gone by since then, but still he told the bear that some day, when his fortune was made, he would release him back to the wild.

In Campden they'd amble down to the marketplace pursued by a throng of children. The gadular would choose a spot not too close to the food stalls. He'd lengthen the chain with a rope, station himself on the stool one of the market women would bring him, and lift his bow to the strings and play. When the shimmering, unearthly music resounded from the gadulka the bear would rise on his hind legs and dance. After, the man would pass round the hat for the coppers and the market traders would bring scraps for the bear. A dancing bear brought extra custom, so everyone was happy.

Thus they plied their trade round the markets, mops, fairs, and wakes of the Cotswolds, even as far as Stratford and Oxford. It was a hard life, especially in winter, when lodgings were cold and food was scarce. But the open road was the only life the Gypsy had ever known. As for the bear, he did as he was bid; he travelled beside his master, he danced, ate, slept, and in his dreams he ranged the wild mountains where he was born.

There came a summer that was too wet, so the corn harvest was poor and the hay left to rot in the meadows; and then a winter unusually harsh. The snow lay deep on the hills for weeks. Up in Stow it was piled up in the streets in great mounds. The early lambs died, some ewes died too, and there was a shortage of turnips and greens in the markets. Folk had little of anything to give beggars or entertainers.

It was late February when the gadular and his bear trudged down Westington Hill. The bear was so thin he looked like a huge shaggy dog. The man was thin too and walked with a stoop and an uncertain step. He'd caught a chill one night they'd had to spend in the open. A head cold and dripping nose had become an ugly rattling in the chest.

At Conduit House he had to crack the ice before they could drink. When they reached Heavenly Corner the cottager agreed to waive the rent till they'd earned some money. In Campden's marketplace, pickings were as thin as everywhere. The poor bear hardly had the strength to rise on his hind legs. But it was the man whose strength gave out. The gadulka suddenly dropped with a clang as the Gypsy fell off the stool, coughing and choking as if he'd never stop.

A clutch of townsmen bundled man and bear back to their lodgings. A doctor was called and did what he could, which was precious little save a bib of gin. The townsfolk brought what broth and greens they could spare. An extra blanket was found to tuck up the Gypsy on his straw bed. The bear cuddled up close to share the warmth of his flea-riddled flank.

It was too little too late. Three days later the gadular passed away. The bear was the only one with him when he died. There ensued a debate about whether the Gypsy was Christian enough to be buried in the churchyard. To hedge his bets, the vicar put him in the far corner beyond the yews.

What, though, to do about the bear? The animal sat sad and lonely in the outhouse. The gadular had been his mother, his father, his only friend. He would tug his chain as far as it would go and peer up the road to the hillside. Perhaps he remembered his master's promise and thought now was the time he'd be set free. But the people of Campden couldn't have a bear loose in the countryside, preying on sheep and menacing milkmaids. Something had to be done soon. In such a time of dearth they couldn't spare him food if he didn't earn his keep. The cottager wanted back his outhouse, and the stink of dung got worse each day because no one dared take the bear to the midden.

Then a party of Gypsies came through town with their ponies and carts. The townsfolk kept their children indoors and watched from their windows as they whispered the old rumours about a people they didn't understand. But the cottager on Heavenly Corner knew the chance must be seized.

'This yere nanimal as I has were once the property to one on your folk.'

The Gypsy men listened with hawkish eyes and said nothing.

'He do dance capital well and I'll give you a good price on him,' sallied the cottager.

The Gypsies pretended not to have heard. One of them spat on the ground. They could use a dancing bear, but they could see that the cottager's need to get shot of the beast was greater than their need to have it. They were doing him a favour by taking it off his hands. As they led him away on his chain the bear looked down Blind Lane, across the Cam valley, a quick glance at Conduit House, as if remembering better days.

Among the Gypsies, as among any people, there are some with softer hearts than others. The father and son who took possession of the bear were hardbitten men who'd suffered much from gadjo prejudice and had little sentiment to spare for animals except their best horses. The son could play the fiddle. The bear's job was to dance. But the music was different from what he was used to and so was the man. When he wouldn't dance they thrashed him. He pined for his old master who would speak to him with soft words. He pined for food too. He was still thin as a dog and his new masters had little food to share. At the Horse Fair that spring they made a great to-do of fiddling and thrashing till at last he rose on his hind legs and the crowd cheered. But the tune wasn't right and he had no heart for dancing. Down he crashed, too weak to stand again however hard they whipped him.

In Campden no one knew for sure the bear's final fate. Some said he turned savage and had to be shot; others that he died of a broken heart. The following February, when again the snow lay hard and white on the hills, strange reports began to come from the vicinity of Heavenly Corner and Blind Lane. Glimpses after dark of a shaggy shape snuffling about with slow, shambling steps. Dogs would flee yelping to the other end of town. The sightings continued over the years. As late as the twentieth century that shambling shape was seen near where the bear and the gadular had slept side by side, walked down Blind Lane, beheld the view across the hills, and the man had promised the bear that someday he'd wander wild and free.

14

THE TEMPLAR KNIGHT

Jerusalem was lost. Acre was lost. Cyprus was lost. It was 1305 and Sir Aldred, a Templar Knight, had come home to England after long years fighting for Christendom under the hot Mediterranean sun. The English summer air seemed chill to him as he rode along Akeman Street to his new home at the preceptory in Quenington. It was easily the grandest building in the village and he rode through the huge gateway with his head held high, keen not to betray the unease he felt at this new, civilian life.

The Preceptor was a perceptive man, however. He saw how Aldred paced the lanes, how he practised over and over with his weapons, how he rode out on Akeman Street to race his horse. So he told him to get acquainted with the nearby manors, and the nobles with whom he'd be working; first the manors that Quenington Preceptory managed, like Wishanger near Stroud, and then the local manors of Coln St Aldwyns and Hatherop.

It was at Hatherop that Aldred's life changed. The tenant, de Handles, was away when he arrived to pay his respects, so he was welcomed by the lady of the manor in the family's private chamber, the solar. There, amid the embroidery and bright silks and the perfume, he saw her. Mirabel, the daughter of the house, her mother's helpmeet and her father's treasure. She was a perfect jewel of young womanhood, bright-faced, with blue eyes that flashed him a curious glance then were modestly lowered. Aldred was instantly captivated. He'd never met a woman like this, so fresh and innocent and good. He hardly knew what to think of these new feelings, but he couldn't keep away. Even though he knew he should.

Every day he could spare – and some he couldn't – he went up through the woods to the manor on the hill, where he would tell his tales of war and the exotic East, and Mira would listen with wide eyes. Her parents welcomed him; he was a nobleman, a Templar, an important land agent, so how could they not? And he was safe, they believed, bound by a rule of poverty, piety, obedience, and – most importantly – chastity. But under his chaste white robes Aldred burned for Mira.

In whispered conversations he told her of his passion and she told him how she returned his feelings. They were young and full of dreams of how one day Aldred would be freed from his religious vows and go into service with the King. They convinced themselves that their hopes would come true, though Aldred was a sworn monk, and told themselves their love was pure even as they stole ardent glances when Mira's mother's back was turned.

Her parents turned a blind eye, but the Preceptor saw the truth. He knew he should chastise his brother in Christ, forbid him to see the girl, but he did nothing. He had guessed that the Templars' days were numbered. It was too late for an old man like him to start again, but if the order ended then a good marriage might be Aldred's best hope for success and happiness.

This happiness was not to be. Mira fell ill. Aldred was distraught and prayed by her bedside day in and day out. His prayers seemed to fall on deaf ears, for Mira grew worse, not better, wasting away as the leaves began to fall from the trees.

This, surely, was a punishment from God for their forbidden love. Aldred entreated God to punish him, not his beloved, but worse and worse she got until all feared for her life. Aldred prayed day and night in the church at Quenington, gazing up at the icon of the Virgin above the altar. He begged for forgiveness for his unclean thoughts, but he couldn't deny he loved Mira and he prayed for the Virgin's understanding and intercession. He swore to dedicate himself to a true holy life if the Holy Mother would cure his beloved.

He would forsake Mira, he swore, and let her marry another, if only she might live. One day, as he came out of the church, he turned and saw above the north porch the brightly painted tympanum showing Christ harrowing the worthy out of hell and away from the Devil. Surely Christ would have mercy on his beloved, for all their sinful feelings, and deliver her from her sickness.

Everyone in the area knew of Mira's illness. Unbeknownst to Aldred, the Preceptor had already written to his brother preceptors and the granges for advice, thinking they might have knowledge of medicine from the East. At length, a letter came from the little grange at Cowley, near Oxford, which offered words of hope. The Preceptor left the letter for Aldred in his cell.

It was late when Aldred returned, exhausted from prayer and despair, but when he read the letter his heart lifted. It spoke of a holy well in Oxford, a healing well dedicated to St Winifred, and said that if a maid drank the waters of this well, then, no matter how sick she was, God would heal her.

Aldred didn't waste a moment. He found a silver flask and stoppered it tight and, although it was nigh on midnight, went straight to the stables and saddled up his grey mare. He led her through the great gateway – and for a moment they both stood there, his white surcoat and her pale coat gleaming in the light of the newly risen moon – and then they were off. He forded the Coln just below Hatherop and saw the faint glow of light from the manor on the hill. He swore that he would not rest until Mira had drunk the holy water and that then he would leave her and be a true monk; then he plunged on again, on to Akeman Street, whose straight, tree-lined route carried him fast towards his goal.

At first the bright moonlight guided his way between the autumn's leaf-shorn trees, but as the night deepened so the clouds gathered. In the darkness he mistook the way and deviated from the road into the woods. At first he noticed nothing amiss. The grey mare raced just as fast along the wide forest rides between pollarded trees. The forest was neat and tidy; not a twig or leaf was wasted by rich or poor. A fine place for hunting deer or grazing pigs. A safe place for a nobleman to be, even so close to midnight.

Slowly, though, and imperceptibly, the forest changed. The mare's hooves sank into deep moss and stumbled over creeping roots. Branches whipped at Aldred's face. The night grew darker and darker. He slowed the horse and squinted into the darkness and, as he did so, the moon came out again, revealing the huge shapes of squat old trees, dripping with moss, their branches low and snaking across every path. He turned and turned again. This wildwood stretched as far as the moonlight let him see; no pollards, no paths, only ferns and twisting branches that seemed to writhe in the half-light.

A light appeared, and then another. The mare trembled. A glowing mist wove through the trees, closing man and horse in from every side. In the stillness of the air he heard faint laughter among the trees. The mare was poised to bolt, but now that the mist had closed around them there was nowhere to run.

Out of the fog arose figures, human-like, but as insubstantial as the mist. Long-limbed they were and tangle-haired, with faces cold and blank, and unseeing empty eyes. With arms outstretched, with grasping, clawing hands, they reached for him. Aldred's hand went to his sword, then twitched away. What good would a sword do against such spectres of the night? If they were demons come to take his soul to hell, then fighting would do him no good. His poor mare danced this way and that to seek escape, but still the mist drew closer.

He gritted his teeth as the chill tendrils of mist reached him, but, just as those shadowy hands seemed about to touch his skin, a shriek rang through the forest and the creatures melted back cowering into the mist. There was but a moment's respite before another figure glided through the seething mass of spirits like a knife through water. She stood out among them like the bright splash of a toadstool on the forest floor, red lips bright on ghastly white skin, raven hair lifting and swirling in a breeze of its own making, and fevered blue eyes boring straight into his soul. All his dreams of Mira, born of hot summer nights, of twisting and turning in his narrow cot, rose up in his mind, and the woman smiled as if she saw all his imaginings laid naked before her.

'My ardent holy knight,' she purred, 'how hot your blood burns under that white surcoat.'

His breath stopped as she reached out to him, and she was cold, colder than the mist, colder than ice, freezing him to the spot as she cooed to him: 'Come to me, my lover, come to me, red cross knight, lie down in the forest and be with me ...' Her glowing eyes compelled him closer. Her fingers caressed the silver flask hanging from his belt.

Aldred's knees grew weak as he yearned towards her, the pulse of his desire was hot under his skin, and she was leaning in, her lips pouting to kiss. Then in his mind's eye he saw Christ leaning over the prone body of Satan above the Quenington church door. The spell was suddenly broken. With a shout of 'In nomine Patris et Filii et Spiritus Sancti,' he wrenched his good steel sword from its scabbard. The woman gave a screeching cry, and as she shot away he saw the outline of bones under her spectral skin, and his throat filled with bile. He swung his sword, slicing through the mist until he saw the bright moon overhead. Then the grey mare sprang away through the trees as if the Devil were at her back.

They heard behind them the shrieking and wailing of the spirits, but they pressed on without a backward glance, the mare's hooves dancing over roots and ferns until at last they saw the moon shining on the Gloucester to London road. Aldred pushed the mare on as fast as she could go, sticking carefully now to the road. They crossed the Windrush at Standlake and again by the swine ford at Eynsham, where, as the first grey fingers of dawn streaked the sky, they saw the spires of Oxford below them.

It was full light by the time Aldred rode through the town to Holywell Manor. The little church of St Cross and the village green close by all seemed so calm that the phantoms of the night were finally swept from his mind. Between the church and the manor stood a little stone structure, and there, as if waiting for him, was a monk. The grey mare was led away on trembling legs. Aldred too felt shaky as the monk beckoned him down steep steps to a rude stone basin beside an icon in the cool, damp chamber. The knight fell to his knees and let the peace and the calm fill him and cleanse away the terror of the night. He prayed long to St Winifred and the Virgin for Mira and for his own imperilled soul. The monk filled his flask with the precious water, and blessed him, and then it was time to be away.

Aldred left his good grey mare to be sent to the Templar grange at Cowley. He was given a chestnut mount with a long, loping gait that ate up the miles. He kept well clear of the woods. In the bright daylight the long night ride already seemed a dark dream. With every mile he drew nearer to Hatherop his heart tightened with fear for his love. The weighty flask by his side bore all his hope.

By nightfall he was there. Up to the solar he went, the flask clutched tight in his hands. He could hardly bear to see his love, her face so gaunt and sunken, but her eyes were trusting and full of love as he told of the holy well and unstoppered the flask. He held it for her to drink and, after, he thought he saw a brightness in her eyes and a flush in her cheeks, and he dared to hope.

His hope proved false. That very night, while he kept a vigil in the manor's hall, his sweetheart Mira died. Her mother, weeping, said that she had just held on long enough to see him again. Numb and empty, Aldred rode back to Quenington. Once he reached his cell he broke down. The Preceptor came rushing when he heard the cries, but there was nothing he could do to soothe the knight's grief.

For days Aldred raved in madness as the guilt and horror pressed upon him that it was all his fault that Mira was dead. At last the monks carried him to the church. They took him in through the south door and there, on the south porch tympanum, he saw the Virgin crowned by her Son, and in his mind he saw Mira in heaven crowned by Christ and taking her place among the blessed. The vision comforted him. He was calmer when they brought him home again.

But that night he had a dreadful dream that he was back in the dark wood among the snaking trees. Leering above him was that livid spectre, her blood red lips parting in a ghastly smile.

'It was I who killed her, red cross knight,' she hissed. 'While you were in my power, I poisoned your precious bottle. Your holy water didn't cure, it killed, and you were to blame, to blame, to blame ...'

He woke with the words ringing in his head. He was to blame that his beloved was dead! If only he hadn't loved her and longed for her! If only he hadn't strayed from the path! If only he hadn't let the woman of the wood so close to him! Sweet Mirabel was dead and he had no will to live without her. It wasn't long till he too fell ill and faded from this mortal world.

The tearful Preceptor buried him in the churchyard and prayed over his grave. Sir Aldred's demise was but another nail in the Templars' coffin. In 1312 the order was banned and the knights dispersed. No one was left in Quenington to remember Aldred or tend his grave and he was forgotten.

Yet travellers must still beware if they roam out at night along the line of Akeman Street. Stray off the path into the tiny surviving scraps of wood and perhaps you too will be lured into the wildwood, for it is still there, hidden in your darkest desires, where the spectral lady with the fevered eyes is waiting to corrupt your dreams.

15

SNOWSHILL MANOR

S nowshill Manor was pretty rundown when Charles Paget Wade bought it in 1919. It had been a grand country house in the sixteenth and seventeenth centuries, but in the nineteenth it was owned by a succession of absentee landlords and occupied by tenant farmers. Wade needed a big house to accommodate the great number of handcrafted objects he'd been collecting since childhood. He hired twenty-eight workmen to renovate the manor, gave them lodgings in the attic rooms, but after the very first night they refused

to sleep there again. There was a creepy feeling up there, said one. There were creaks and footsteps on the stairs, and whispers in the darkness. One man heard a melody of old-fashioned music from the room below his. Others heard the clashing of steel blades.

So Wade had to find them digs elsewhere, some of them in the Snowshill Arms just along the road. But the inn was haunted too. Dogs were most sensitive to it. They'd suddenly start snarling, even howling, and then back off in terror with their tail between their legs. Doors would open by themselves. Sometimes a burly hooded figure was glimpsed upstairs. The ghost of a monk, they said; an angry one. The same scowling figure had also been seen on the stairs in the manor and haunted the stretch of road past the manor and the pub. Some folk in the village wouldn't pass there after dark, and horses pulling carts often came to a stop and refused to go on.

Why a monk? And why was he so angry? Long ago the manor estate had belonged to Winchcombe Abbey. Some say there was a priory where the manor now stands, and accommodation in what's now the Snowshill Arms for monks who'd come to inspect the estate and collect rents. But in 1539 Winchcombe Abbey was closed, its stone pillaged, its monks dispersed, its lands confiscated. Snowshill Manor became the property of the King, who passed it into private hands. Maybe the monk was angry because of the ways that times had changed. Wade understood that feeling all too well.

But how could the ghost of a dispossessed Benedictine monk explain the sound of clashing swords, the ghostly music, the top-hatted figure of a nineteenth-century gentleman glimpsed in the grounds after dark? From studying objects from all over the world, Wade had learnt to be open-minded. He sent some wood from a beam under the rooms where the workmen had slept to a woman in Brighton who had some reputation as a seer. As this woman attended upon the fragment of beam she fell into a trance. She knew nothing of Snowshill or its history, but in her trance she saw a big house and in an upper room, late at night, a young woman dressed in a green gown of seventeenth-century cut. The girl was pacing up and down, wringing her hands, saying, 'I do not want to stay the night.'

Wade had no idea what to make of that. But he soon heard a story that perhaps shed light on the identity of the top-hatted gentleman. It came from an old fellow who'd married the daughter of a farm labourer called Richard Carter. Back in the 1850s Carter had been a trusted employee of Charles Marshall, the manor's tenant at that time. After Marshall's death in 1858, his widow continued to farm the estate and Carter remained in her employ. One evening, Carter had to work late at Hill Barn Farm, half a mile up the Campden road. He was walking back to the village in the dark when he heard hoof beats behind him. He quickened his step. The hoof beats came faster. He glanced back. A man on a black horse. Wearing a top hat. When the rider drew alongside Carter, the workman saw it was Charles Marshall, dead these many months. Carter yelped in terror and broke into a run, the ghostly horseman pounding along behind till they neared the church. The same thing happened on a different road the next time Carter was out after dark. It happened again and again, till he was terrified of going anywhere after sundown and resorted to speaking to the rector.

'It seems to me', said the rector, 'that Mr Marshall's spirit wants you to do something for him. The next time you see him, you should ask, "In the name of the Lord, what troublest thou?"'

Two evenings later Carter dared to be out late and heard once again the spectral hooves. He held his ground as the horseman rode up to him and stared at him with deep-shadowed eyes.

'In the n-name of the Lord, w-what troublest thou?'

With a voice like gravel the horseman said, 'Meet me in the chaff-house at midnight.'

Shortly before midnight, with his heart in his mouth, Carter stole down to the chaff-house in the farmyard below the manor. There the top-hatted figure appeared to him on foot and handed him a folded note.

'See that Mrs Marshall gets this,' came the dry rattling voice. 'I should have told her long ago.'

With that the ghost was gone. Carter was not a lettered man, so he couldn't read the note, but after Marshall's widow had seen it she took him into her confidence. The note directed her to a hidden location in the manor, where she found a hoard of gold coins and jewellery. They say that's how she was able to fund the building work she undertook over the next few years.

But where had that gold come from in the first place?

As Wade pressed on with renovating the manor, his collections continued to expand. He had toys, ornaments, furniture; weapons and armour; bicycles, looms, spinning wheels; clocks, tools, pictures; musical instruments of every kind. He was driven to collect by his love of the fine craftsmanship he feared was vanishing from the world. To ordinary folk, though, his obsession seemed strange. His hair was weirdly long. He had no wife. People whispered about the objects pertaining to magic and witchcraft that he kept in an attic room he called 'The Witch's Garrett'. Some said he sought to work magic up there. Was his purpose, perhaps, to lay the ghosts of this old house?

For the hauntings continued. From the room Wade called 'Zenith' clashing swords could still be heard. He heard a story that two men once fought a duel in that room and one of them died from his wounds. The reason for the duel was unknown. A woman who worked in the house kept hearing footsteps pacing past her upstairs room, but if she opened the door there'd be no one there. And then, some years after his correspondence with the Brighton seer, Wade saw papers concerning a case brought to the Star Chamber in 1604 which made the vision of the girl in green fall into place.

At the beginning of 1604 Ann Parsons of Overbury in Worcestershire was fifteen years old. Her parents were dead but her mother had left an estate worth a thousand marks which Ann would inherit when she reached the age of sixteen or got married. Her guardian, Richard Daston, adroitly arranged her engagement to the son, George, of his half-brother Sir William Savage. While George was working in London, Ann went to live under Sir William's roof at Elmley Castle. A servant there, named Anthony Palmer, took advantage of this hiatus to court Ann with promises of a splendid house and lands. He had no fortune of his own and was all too eagerly aware of hers. His sister, confusingly called Anne, helped to win the girl's trust, telling her how much Anthony loved her and what a fine life they could have.

On St Valentine's Eve, when Sir William was away, Anthony Palmer and Ann Parsons eloped. Only it wasn't quite as romantic as that sounds. When the household was abed Anthony slipped down to open the doors to the gang of his mates waiting outside with horses. His sister Anne went to Ann's room to make sure she was ready. Now the moment was upon her, young Ann wasn't at all sure she should go.

'It will be well,' Anne Palmer whispered. 'Let us be quick! Thy bridegroom is waiting.'

Anthony hurried back upstairs to see what was keeping them. In the coming and going, the steward was awoken. Scuffling broke out with Sir William's loyal serving men as Anthony's friends forced their way in and Anthony and his sister secured the portable part of young Ann's dowry. With knives and staves the intruders held back Sir William's men while the brother and sister hustled Ann and her bags of gold out to the horses.

The party rode first to the Palmers' family home in Broadway. They didn't linger in so obvious a refuge. Soon they were riding on, the horses' breath frosting in the chill night air, till they reached Snowshill Manor. The manor was owned then by John Warren, whose brother had married a cousin of Ann Parsons. He must have thought he was doing Ann a favour. The priest who'd been summoned, the Reverend Richard Stone, also took a romantic view of the situation: the elopement by night, the midnight ceremony in an upstairs room, the courtly tune that one of Anthony's friends played on a recorder, the young bride in her green silk dress, lisping the vows she was called upon to make.

A room had been readied for the couple's first night of wedded bliss. But already Ann was having second thoughts. She paced up and down, wringing her hands, saying, 'I do not want to stay the night.' There was something creepy about this house, about the whole situation. She wished she wasn't here. She wanted her poor dead mother.

Her anxiousness put her new husband on edge. He was nervous too what Sir William would do when he found out. The more Anthony thought about it, the surer he knew that the old man would come after them. His impulse was to flee yet further from Elmley Castle. It was agreed that Ann's gold should for now be kept at Snowshill; it would be safer there, in one of the manor's hidey-holes, and John Warren's loyalty to Ann was certain. The Palmers' party rode on through the night to lodgings in Chipping Campden.

Sir William's spies in the countryside did their work. At Campden he caught up with the fugitives. When they saw his retainers' swords Anthony and his friends quickly fled into the night and the young bride was recaptured.

Sir William ascertained the hostelry bed had not been slept in and asked her bluntly, 'Hast thou given thy body to that scallywag?'

With downcast eyes she whispered, 'Nay.'

'Then 'tis no true marriage, my lass. Thou shalt yet be wed to my son.'

Owing to the legal complexities of the situation, he hid her in the care of her grandmother not far from Elmley Castle at Sedgeberrow. But Anthony Palmer's grit proved tougher than Sir William expected. Anthony discovered Ann's location and abducted her a second time. The elderly granny put up a stout resistance and for her pains got a beating – and a dagger blow through her hand.

Palmer's cause was hopeless. All the power and privilege of rank weighed against him. Soon enough the law caught up with him and his confederates, who were arraigned before the Star Chamber on charges of abduction and unlawful marriage. Anne Palmer was accused of having orchestrated the plot. She insisted that Ann Parsons had departed willingly from Elmley Castle with her brother and that neither he nor she had any knowledge Ann was engaged to George Savage.

The outcome of the proceedings is lost. No one knows whether the secret marriage in Snowshill Manor was annulled. All that's recorded of Ann Parsons thereafter is that by the time of her death in 1682 her name was Ann Clarke. Did she find in the end a man who loved her for who she was instead of for her wealth?

And what happened to Ann's gold squirrelled away in Snowshill Manor? Perhaps it stayed there, unretrieved, till a century later someone got wind of it, thought they had claim to it, dug it out from its hidey-hole, but someone else disagreed and so a duel ensued. Hence the clashing of swords, the fatal thrust, a man bleeding out his life upon the floor. And so the gold remained there, till Charles Marshall, who'd never got round to telling his wife, returned from his grave.

When Charles Wade had learnt the truth of the girl in green, he named the room in which her marriage took place 'Ann's Room'. The girl's distress in that midnight hour was seared into the fabric of that room. Ever afterwards her spirit would pace up and down. The story fascinated Wade's guests, some of whom dared to stay overnight in the room. One young woman said she felt a presence of someone innocent and anxious. She saw no apparition but heard a few notes of music wafting from the 'Music Room' next door.

Five years before his death in 1956, Wade handed over the manor and his collections to the National Trust. The magic and witchcraft objects must have seemed too scary, because they were transferred to the Museum of Witchcraft in Boscastle. How seriously Wade took the magic I don't know, but if he tried to lay the ghosts of Snowshill it didn't work. They're all still there, the accumulation of spectres that old buildings gather like dust. The Benedictine monk, still haunting the pub, sometimes climbing the stairs in the manor, intent on collecting monies his order is no longer entitled to, still angry at all that's changed. Young Ann Parsons in her green wedding dress, pacing up and down, not wanting to stay the night. The duellists in Zenith endlessly propelled into deadly combat. Top-hatted Charles Marshall heading down to the farmyard. And now another ... footsteps in the rooms after the visitors have gone ... the ghost of Charles Paget Wade doing his rounds to keep an eye on his precious collections.

16

THE WOMAN'S WRAITH

Martha Legg pulled her shawl tight around her shoulders as she left her parents' cottage and walked quickly away from Kempsford's village green. The thatched cottages away from the road were wreathed in mist, and the sky above was the deep blue of very early morning. The only person about at this hour, she envied those able to lie in a little longer in the autumn. She still had to go to the fields. Money was money. Every penny earned made her engagement to Ned Coule a little more likely.

She walked down to the swing bridge and exchanged a weary smile with the bridge keeper as she crossed over the canal to walk along the towpath. Soon she was out of the village and into the fields. It was brighter now, grey light filling the sky, but a white mist yet clung to the still waters of the canal. Martha shivered as the moisture seeped through her woollen shawl. The newly risen sun was struggling to break through the mist here on the canal, but straight ahead it was shining on the brickwork of Oatlands Bridge, turning it a vivid red, the brightest colour in the flat autumn landscape of brown fields and almost bare trees. Walking in a tunnel of whiteness, Martha had a sudden feeling of being trapped. The sun shining into the mist made it bright, almost blinding.

She walked on with quick steps. If the sun was coming out, maybe the day wouldn't be too bad after all. She looked up again to the bridge, and frowned. Below the arch on the near side the mist was very thick – and it was flowing and shifting about. She scrubbed at her eyes. When she looked again the mist was coalescing … a misty form was rising up from the water, a form that was … almost human. It hung there by the towpath, just short of being under the bridge.

It seemed to be waiting.

Martha's breath caught in her throat as she swallowed the impulse to scream. She rubbed her eyes again, but the thing was still there, still and silent. She took a step back without meaning to and, heart pounding, felt a rush of need to turn tail and run back to the village. But what would she say? A foolish tale about a bugaboo by the bridge would lose her this hard-won job. It was surely just a trick of the light.

She took a deep breath and walked on, but, although the mist was clearing off the water, the figure didn't go away. It just hung there, its misty form shifting as if a breeze had caught it, yet the air was completely still. She really didn't want to walk past it, but she had no choice if she wanted to get to work. She dropped her gaze to her feet and held her breath as she walked on towards the bridge. She could still see the figure's hazy legs drifting over the water by the towpath. Her resolve began to weaken.

Keep your eyes on the path! By the time she reached the bridge all she could see was the muddy track in front of her. If she couldn't see it, then perhaps it wasn't there. A child's logic, but all she had to cling to. Going under the arch, she reached out to touch the cold

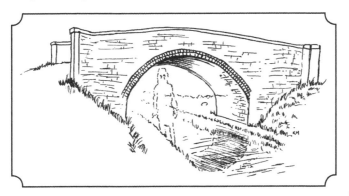

but reassuringly solid bricks. She had to keep walking on. But she couldn't quite stop herself glancing slightly to the right, to check she was past the figure. Her breath caught again and she almost fell. Right beside her, as if it was pacing her, were the thing's misty legs. With the next step she glanced again and the figure was again beside her. Without making a conscious decision, she began to run. She was out from the bridge in a flash, legs pounding, and on into the morning light. But she couldn't run for ever. She slowed, chest heaving, and her head traitorously turned to the right again. For a moment she thought she'd outrun it. Then the misty legs drifted into view beside her once more.

Ahead was the entrance to the field where she worked. She heaved a great breath and ran again. If this was a thing of the water, surely it couldn't follow her across the land? She turned from the towpath and stepped into the muddy field. A quick backward glance. It was there. Right behind her. An eyeless thing of white swirling mist, only inches from her face. A ragged scream tore from her throat. The air expelled from her mouth shifted the misty form, but soon it recoalesced. She turned away, gasping. There was no escape. She understood that now. All she could do was endure. She went about her work, pulling up swedes, giving them a quick scrub down, chucking them into piles to be collected later.

The ghostly figure was constantly by her side.

Pulling swedes is heavy, backbreaking work, but usually she enjoyed the solitude it brought, away from her parents' house and the clamour of her younger siblings. Today she'd have given anything to hear their voices. All day long she saw not a soul. No voice rose in greeting from the path. No heavy clop of horse's hooves. No swoosh of a boat passing by. Only the silent figure of mist kept her company.

As the day passed she sank into a weary lassitude. A dull pain lodged itself in her chest. Her limbs felt like lead as she hauled the swedes. She didn't dare think, but a small part of her mind panicked every time she caught a glimpse of the misty form.

At last the lengthening shadows told her it was time to go home. It was no surprise that the figure followed her to the towpath and paced her as she trudged back towards the bridge. In the gathering gloom she imagined it following her all the way home and hovering above her in her bed that night. Now she was at the bridge, dark and forbidding in the failing light. She stepped into its shadow and walked quickly through, looking nowhere but straight down at the ground in front of her.

She went quite a few steps beyond the bridge before she had the nerve to glance to her left. She saw only the dark water of the canal. The thing was gone from beside her. She didn't dare look back. She jumped when the village church began to ring the bells for seven o'clock. She looked towards the village, blinking in the fading light. Such a distance she had yet to walk! Still she didn't look behind her, but she could feel a prickling on the back of her neck.

It was a slow slog home, never looking back. She didn't answer the bridge keeper's smile as she crossed back into the village. When she got home her mother was dishing up the tea, but Martha couldn't eat. As soon as the things were cleared away she took to her bed.

The next day she wouldn't get out of it; just lay there, staring at the wall. Her mother sent for the doctor, then for young Ned Coule, but neither could rouse her. After a week her mother had to call the vicar. While he sat beside her, Martha whispered out her tale. 'I do warrant, reverend, as that bugaboo were my own spirit, like, a-calling me away.'

It seemed that was true, as that very same day she died.

Oatlands Bridge is an even lonelier place today. The canal is long gone, and the bridge overgrown and desolate, marooned in a field down a private path. There's no water there now from which a form might rise like the one Martha saw, but on misty days perhaps it's best to stay away.

17

THE GIBBET ON DURDHAM DOWN

Clifton Down seems benign enough today with its strolling students and its well-to-do ladies walking their dogs. It wasn't like that two hundred years ago, especially in the area above Pembroke Road once known as Gallows Acre. The whole expanse of downland between Clifton and Westbury on Trym was called Durdham Down back then and extended southwards where grand Victorian houses stand today. Its paths twisted and turned through gorse, bramble, and bracken as high as your chin. In the more open parts, sheep wandered and grazed. In those days much of England's landscape was a Boschian nightmare bristling with gallows and crow-pecked gibbets. So it was on Durdham Down, where gibbets creaked as their grisly cargo swung to and fro, and undeterred ruffians stalked unwary travellers.

In this habitat lurked an unfortunate Welshman called Shenkin Protheroe. They call him the 'dwarf highwayman', but really he was a beggar, crippled by polio, his legs reduced to useless appendages, so he had to haul himself along by means of his long, powerful arms and a pair of little hand stools. He would sit by the lanes and scrounge his living from the traffic of passers-by.

One morning at winter's end in 1783, Shenkin was shivering in his rags by Gallows Acre Lane, as Pembroke Road was then known, near the spot where today a stone tower holds an air shaft to the railway tunnel beneath. A pig drover came by, Evan

Daniel by name, herding five young swine to market in Bristol. Shenkin flaunted his withered legs and crooned his plea for coin, and Evan took out a leather purse and threw him some coppers. In the moments when the purse was open, Shenkin glimpsed the sparkle of something brighter than copper. For the rest of the day he couldn't get the thought of it out of his mind. He was a villain, for sure, but think how he became one: an outcast without family, unable to walk or work, who'd endured winter in the open air, surviving on the coppers of charity and scraps of discarded food.

Shenkin guessed the drover would come back the same way when he'd delivered the swine. So the beggar lingered by that spot, pleading for coppers as other people trudged by, but thinking all the time of silver and gold. At dusk he spied Evan Daniel making his way back up the lane. Shenkin had a plan. He heaved himself with his strong arms into a ditch, waited till the footsteps drew near, then began to moan piteously.

Evan hurried over to see who was there.

'I fell in,' moaned Shenkin, 'and I can't get me out on account of me legs.'

Carefully the drover climbed down into the ditch. The moment he stooped to help the stricken man, Shenkin reached up one powerful arm and grasped his throat and with his other hand pulled out a knife. Who knows whether he intended to kill? In the struggle the blade went into Evan's heart and down he fell, bleeding out his life into the mud.

Shenkin rifled through the dead man's clothes till he found the purse. There was silver, no gold, not a prince's fortune, but a fortune to a beggar. He didn't think to separate the coins from the purse; he stuffed the whole thing into his shirt and levered himself out of the ditch and away through the shadows, his useless legs dragging along behind.

He didn't get far. When the hue and cry went up, people reported seeing Shenkin close to where the body was found. The constables scoured the down and caught him in the woods near the river. The purse they found on him put the prosecution's case beyond challenge. They hanged him first, then tarred his body

to make it last longer than unprotected flesh, and mounted it in an iron cage dangling from a gibbet erected near the spot where Evan Daniel was murdered.

This ghastly spectacle stood in full view of Gallows Acre Lane and the track to Westbury. It was there for years. The crows teased gobbets of flesh from under the tar. The ragged clothes frayed away. Soon there was little more than a skeleton held together by gristle salted by the wind off the Bristol Channel and kept upright by the cage. The cage would swing on its chain and the bones rattle against the bars as the wind whistled through. Such terrifying noises in the dark. So stories began to grow of the moanings and whisperings, of shadows among the shadows; the rumour that Shenkin descended by night from his cage and lurched through the thickets upon his long, skeletal arms.

The good folk of Westbury were so afraid of passing that spot after dark that when they had to come back late from Bristol, especially when the nights closed in, they would wait at Richmond Hill till others of their neighbours who'd been in town arrived there. Only when their number attained a critical mass of courage would they proceed up Gallows Acre Lane and past Shenkin's gibbet.

Among these Westbury folk was a farmer by the name of Rudge. He was quite well-to-to and self-satisfied to be so. He had a wife who obeyed him and a daughter called Jenny who was a rare piece with sparkling eyes and a quick smile. She enjoyed the attention of the apprentice lads and, left to herself, she'd have had some fun and no doubt quickly ended up married. But Farmer and Mistress Rudge weren't ready to let her go. She was old enough to be useful, and young enough to wait, and Farmer Rudge was sure that no apprentice boy could be worthy of his precious daughter.

But you can't stop the forces of nature. In spite of all her parents' efforts, Jenny formed an attachment to one Dick Foyle, a hosier's apprentice in a Wine Street shop she visited when she came to Bristol on market days. Snatched words and smouldering glances were all they could manage before her mother would drag her away. Only it was more than a passing fancy. Jenny and Dick were in love. Three years had gone by since Evan Daniel's murder, and Shenkin Protheroe was still swinging in his cage, when Jenny and Dick decided to elope. They communicated by secret notes left in a cucumber frame in the Rudge garden which Dick could reach by stretching over the hedge. Soon their preparations were made. On a Sunday morning in spring, when the Rudges would be at church, Dick slipped a note in the cucumber frame to confirm that Jenny should meet him on the path on Tuesday night.

But Farmer Rudge wasn't at church that morning. Some new cider last night had disagreed with him, so he was dozing by the fire when he heard footsteps past his garden. Thinking of carrot thieves, he peered from the corner of the window and saw Dick Foyle reaching over the hedge to put something in the cucumber frame. Rudge waited till the lad had gone then went to find the note. His fury was incandescent. To think that such lowlife thought he could steal *his* daughter!

Mistress Rudge had orders not to let Jenny out of her sight when, next day, Farmer Rudge went to the shop in Wine Street.

He rapped on the counter with his stout oak staff. 'Listen to me, you counter hopper!' he bawled at Dick. 'You ever come near my premises again and I'll break every bone in your body!'

Dick was shocked but undaunted. His heart was set on Jenny Rudge and he pitied her being trapped under the thumb of such a tyrant. He was all the more determined to take her away. He knew that she still loved him. But for months afterwards he couldn't get anywhere near her. Either her mother or her father stayed with her wherever she went. Whenever Farmer Rudge laid eyes on Dick he stomped the tip of his staff on the ground.

Dick bided his time, made new plans, bought the rope he'd need, and some dark clothes, and practised his gymnastics. In the autumn he was ready. On market day Jenny came to town with her eagle-eyed parents, and in the press of people in the marketplace Dick felt her hand squeeze his tight as he slipped a note in her pocket.

A wind was rising, a storm on the way, and it was already dark as Westbury folk began to congregate at Richmond Hill. There were almost but not quite enough of them to dare the passage of Gallows Acre. Then Farmer Rudge arrived with his stout oak staff and his wife and fair daughter, and the company felt bold enough to proceed.

The wind blew harder. Black and grey clouds scudded across the moon. The older folk toiled on the incline, while younger ones were hurrisome to get past the ordeal of Shenkin's gibbet. As they drew nearer they began to hear the creaking of the chain in the gale, the dry rattle of bones against iron, the whistling of the wind through the unholy instrument made by the skeleton in its cage. The band of people stuck close together, held back by the slowest.

Now they were right by the gibbet. For a few moments the clouds parted and a moonbeam illuminated the cage. Inside it – the horror! – Shenkin's skeleton frantically shook about as if struggling to escape from its prison. There were screams and gasps. The swirling clouds cut off the moonbeam. In the gloom a slender shadow was seen to glide, with an unearthly howl, down from the gibbet cage. Everyone screamed then, even Farmer Rudge with his oaken staff. The good folk scattered, still screaming, every which way across the down.

Farmer Rudge instinctively legged it homewards. His wife kept pace with him. Only when they got as far as the turn to Stoke Bishop did they realise Jenny wasn't with them. They wheeled about, calling for her. Their fears for their daughter tore against the terror of what they'd seen. They stumbled back through the dark and the storm, halfway to the gibbet, yelling Jenny's name. They bumped into some of their erstwhile companions, who came to help search. All to no avail.

Then Mistress Rudge slapped her palm to her brow. 'I tell ee, Mr Rudge, that wench must have runned all the way home!'

So they hurried home to Westbury – and found the house empty. The girl was still out there on Durdham Down, alone in the stormy night, and God knows what out there with her! They lit lanterns and with a posse of neighbours they searched the down till dawn and still they didn't find her. How her parents grieved then! What horror had taken her?

But the reason they couldn't find her was that Dick's bold trick with gibbet and rope had worked a treat and in the pandemonium he'd spirited her away in a smart Whitechapel cart specially borrowed for the occasion. Sunrise brought them to the village of Aust beside the estuary, where Dick's old aunt made them welcome in her humble lodgings. There was talk of taking the ferry across to Beachley and Wales, but the aunt counselled a less drastic course. She found a minister to marry them and then sent them back to Westbury.

Farmer Rudge was furious, but the deed was done and no going back on it. He made the best of a bad job and let the newlyweds stay on the farm. Dick made himself useful and before you could say 'Bristol Bridge' he was managing the place and old Rudge had retired to his fireside and cider. It wasn't too many years before the father and mother passed away and Dick and Jenny became master and mistress of the farm and their own lives. Often they would drive into Bristol and – when it was daylight – laugh as they passed Shenkin Protheroe's whitened bones, still up there on the gibbet, and remembered the trick Dick had played that stormy night to win his heart's desire.

After quite a number of years the authorities finally took down the gibbet. Clifton was expanding and getting prosperous and its well-to-do inhabitants were none too keen that such a spectacle should sully their neighbourhood. Dick secured a piece of wood from the crossbeam on which he'd once precariously stood. He had it made into a tobacco box inscribed 'To the memory of Shenkin Protheroe, Esq.' That tobacco box became an heirloom passed down to Dick and Jenny's descendants, who would tell attentive visitors the story of where it came from.

Dick Foyle may, by means of a rope and agility, have staged the uncanny manifestations of that dark stormy night, but who's to say that Shenkin's unquiet spirit has yet departed from Clifton Down? Strange stories are still heard. In the 1970s an antique dealer was walking her dog after dark near the tower where the gibbet once stood. It was a clear night without a breath of breeze or a tendril of mist. Suddenly her dog started whimpering and she saw a spiral of smoke or vapour weirdly rising from the ground. Was it just a stray emission from a locomotive passing through the tunnel, or was it the ghost of Shenkin Protheroe still haunting the down?

18

THE BLACKSMITH'S REVENGE

Standing in the courtroom in the Bear Inn at Bisley, Tobias Gardiner was furious. He was angry he'd been caught stealing that sheep, yes, but the smooth, smug face of the judge, Sir Charles Coxe, filled him with greater fury. How dare this man, who had never wanted for anything in his life, presume to judge him for trying to feed his family?

Judge Coxe looked back across the courtroom at the man in the dock. What a betrayal of trust! His own employee, a skilled man, trusted to make the intricate gates for his new home. The man couldn't be in need; Coxe hadn't paid him yet, but there was always work for blacksmiths. The dastard was lazy; that was his problem. Coxe saw how Gardiner glared back at him as if he was in the right, as if he had the right to look a gentleman and an employer in the eye! In this year of our Lord 1712 the penalty for sheep-stealing was death. It would be a pleasure to teach this surly man a lesson, Coxe thought, especially since the sheep he had stolen was one of Coxe's own. Yes, string him high! Let him be a lesson to others who might stray.

He was just about to open his mouth to declare that Tobias Gardiner was condemned to die, when a thought struck him. If Gardiner died, then Coxe's gates would be unfinished, and there was no blacksmith as skilled for miles around. Then the idea came to him, and he smiled.

'This man,' Coxe began, 'has been in my employ as a skilled blacksmith.'

The people who'd crowded into the courtroom hissed at that.

'I am minded, therefore, to look leniently on him.'

There was a collective gasp. Very satisfying.

'I will allow Gardiner to complete the gates he is working on for me, and if – but only if – they are flawless, then perhaps I will look more tolerantly on his sentence.'

There were more gasps, some approving, some not. Gardiner stood stock still. He could see the little smile on the judge's face and he knew in his heart exactly what Coxe was playing at. Commute the sentence? Hardly! What he wanted was a set of gates for free, the only cost a man's life. How dare he? Gardiner felt the fury boil up in him again. He was just about to open his mouth to say no, to take his punishment like a man, when he caught a glimpse of his wife's face, her tentative look of relief, and the anger bled out of him. His shoulders slumped and he heard himself agree.

All through Christmas and into cold January, Gardiner sweated over his forge, curling and twisting the iron into the intricate design. The gates were as perfect as he could make them, but the work did nothing to damp the anger in his heart.

Once, shortly before the job was finished, Coxe brought his friends to visit what he called his 'experiment'. The gentry piled into the hot forge, dabbing their faces with their lacy hand-kerchiefs, and Coxe strode around as if he owned the place and ostentatiously inspected the gates.

'Fine work,' said Coxe, that little smile curving the corners of his mouth. 'You see, I like to think of myself as a reformer. They have to learn, these criminal types, that hard work is the only way to get on. They are like children, you know, and have to be taught that you don't get something for nothing.'

Gardiner felt the wrath rise in him like a flame in the forge. Something for nothing? Something for *nothing*? Like Coxe's wealth, his title, and his land? That were his only by a quirk of birth. That little smile promised nothing but death. Something for nothing? That was the gates Gardiner had sweated over these last months.

Something snapped inside him. Damn Coxe if he thought he could have something for nothing! He picked up a gobbet of metal and thrust it into the fire, then dropped the molten glob on to the top right-hand corner, where the fanciest work was. With infinite care he twisted it this way and that until he was satisfied. He smiled grimly to himself. He'd never had a hope and he'd be a fool if he'd ever thought he had.

The January day the gates were to be installed at Nether Lypiatt Manor was icy cold. Coxe pored over the gates while a crowd gathered round and shivered. The cruel little smile was hovering on his face all the while until he came to the flaw. A curlicue – perfectly done – faced in exactly the wrong direction. It couldn't be a mistake, not with the care that had gone into it. He looked up to where Gardiner stood. The blacksmith stared back, as steady as you like, and something passed between the two men in that moment.

Then a hard expression shuttered Coxe's face. He lifted his head and announced to the crowd, 'There is a flaw. A *deliberate* flaw. By such an act of mockery Tobias Gardiner forfeits any right to leniency. He is to be hanged by the neck until he is dead for the stealing of a sheep from the Nether Lypiatt estate.'

On the appointed day, 25 January, as Gardiner waited by the scaffold, he saw his wife weeping and his eldest son standing stoically by her, and he felt the anger rise yet again. When the rope was placed around his neck, he turned to where Judge Coxe was watching with that damn smile still on his face and he said, 'You've not seen the last of me, Judge Coxe. May your house be cursed from this time on into eternity!'

Then the rope tightened and he was hauled high and knew no more of earthly cares.

At first the curse seemed to have no effect. Gardiner's family fell into poverty and had to leave the parish. At Nether Lypiatt the Coxes flourished. The gates were installed, flaw or no, and they opened and closed many times that year. By the end of it the house was complete enough for Coxe to sleep in his fine bed in his fine new manor house. But as 1714 began, a bitter winter brewed. The wind whistled round the house night after night, rattling the roof tiles and wuthering the tall trees Coxe had planted to block that very element.

On the night of 25 January the wind rattled and roared so much that Coxe was kept awake in his bed. It sounded as if there were something out there. Almost the wind sounded like a man's moans and cries, like a man in torment. Beside him, his wife shifted in her sleep. Coxe swung himself out of bed, went to the window, and stepped inside the curtains to look out.

The clouds were scudding fast across the moon. The trees bent before the howling wind. Louder and louder it grew, wailing enough to break a heart. Suddenly, where there had been nothing, a horse and rider stood in the garden below. The horse was white, the rider dark and burly, and both seemed to glow from within. As Coxe watched, the rider turned and looked straight up at him.

With a gasp Coxe fell back, tangling himself in the curtain. Before he could extricate himself the rider turned his steed and galloped to the firmly shut gates. With an almighty crash and clang the gates flew open, the horseman rode through, the horse reared up on his hind legs, the rider shook his fist at Coxe, and then they were gone, vanished into thin air, and the drive was empty again.

Coxe tumbled back through the curtains into the dark bedroom. Outside, the wind had stilled. He leaned back against the wall and stared into space. He'd recognised the rider. It was the blacksmith. Coxe knew then that Gardiner's curse had come to haunt him.

From that time on, Coxe's fortunes began to turn for the worse. He lost his parliamentary seat at the election. When Queen Anne took the throne and a Whig government came in, he lost his position as a judge as well. Belts had to be tightened – a little – at Nether Lypiatt Manor.

And every 25 January the sky would be alive with wails, the blacksmith would come, and the gates would be thrown open. It wasn't just Coxe who saw him, but his wife, his son, his servants too. Long after Sir Charles Coxe's death, the blacksmith continued to visit the manor, reminding the Coxe family that nothing was to be had for nothing in this life. You always had to pay, one way or another. Even after the house passed out of the family's hands in 1884 the ghost kept on coming, the curse was still potent. Even after the gates were restored in the 1920s the ghost was still there, blamed for accidents and divorces, even the death of beloved pets. And some say that even today, on 25 January, the blacksmith rides through the gates of Nether Lypiatt Manor and you can hear his wails in the wind all the way down to Thrupp.

19

THE SHADOW OF THE WORKHOUSE

P eter Rickett used to like his attic room in Stow. He'd sit at his table for hours constructing his Airfix models, and from his gable window he had a view across the shadowy street to the fire station. It was always exciting when the alarm went off and a fire engine roared out, siren blaring. It must have been a bit like that in the war when the air-raid sirens sounded and the Spitfires and Hurricanes scrambled to meet the German bombers.

Next to the fire station was East View, the geriatric hospital – or 'workhouse' as people still called it. With its square cruciform-layout building and its high walls, it looked like a prison. Even from Peter's window it was hard to catch a glimpse of the inmates in the yards. He'd used to pretend it was Colditz, full of Allied airmen trying to tunnel under the walls to the Ricketts' garden. But one day he did see someone. It was the day after his fourteenth birthday and he was testing out his new binoculars, when he saw an old man looking down from an interior window into the yard. The man's face, magnified through the binoculars, looked desperate as a trapped animal's, as if he didn't understand why he was there and couldn't leave. Peter felt troubled by that, in a way he'd never experienced before; but soon enough he forgot about it.

That very night he was woken by a tapping in his wardrobe. He got up and opened the wardrobe and the tapping stopped and his clothes hung innocently on their hangers. But it happened again on other nights. Then a damp patch appeared in his bed. He didn't know how it got there and it was too embarrassing to mention to his parents. Then damp patches appeared in the carpet as well.

One night his chair moved. It had been in its usual place behind his table, but in the morning it was on the other side of the room. That really scared him, but he still dared not talk to his parents. When his mum marched stiffly in and pulled back the covers of his bed to expose the tidemarks on the sheet and said between her teeth, 'Can you do something about this?' he simply turned crimson and said nothing.

The tapping at night got louder. It came not just from the wardrobe but from the tallboy as well, and even the walls. The chair crashed over backwards and the window clattered as if shaken by a gale. Mr Rickett shouted from the landing, 'Do you have to make so much noise?' In the morning there was a soggy patch on the bed again, one of the sheets was ripped, and Peter's dressing gown was no longer on its hook but instead rammed under the mattress. When his mum came in and saw the state of the room, she stared for a moment and then marched out without a word.

That morning Peter took his breakfast to his room to avoid sitting with his parents. It was a Saturday. He wanted to build his new RAF Emergency Set, which comprised an ambulance and a crash tender. Soon the models were assembled and he was absorbed in painting them. He nearly jumped out of his skin when the alarm sounded across the road and one of the fire engines roared screaming out of the station. He'd just started painting the Airfix crash tender when that happened!

A little later his dad came in. He sat gingerly on the bed and for a whole minute was silent. Peter carried on applying red paint as if he hadn't noticed his dad was there.

Mr Rickett cleared his throat. 'You're fourteen now, aren't you, Peter?'

Duh!

'Can we talk for a moment?'

Peter upended his brush in the jam jar of white spirit and turned on his chair. Both of them avoided meeting the other's gaze.

'Peter, I thought maybe it was time we had a little talk about, er, growing up.'

The boy's heart sank. The talk was excruciating and inconclusive. Peter acknowledged that the basics had been covered in Biology. He didn't mention the expansion of his knowledge by James Bond novels.

'If you need to talk about anything, I'm always here.' Duty done, Mr Rickett departed and Peter, still cringing, took up his brush.

The nocturnal activities in Peter's room carried on. The soggy patches on the carpet got larger and coalesced and began to rise up the walls. Sheets of moisture that climbed ever higher, night by night, like condensation from the breath of too many people packed in a hot confined space. So much water that it seemed to defy gravity as it streamed up the walls, great drops then dribbling back down; the windows opaque with it like smoked glass. Mrs Rickett called in the plumber. He couldn't find a leak. He seemed edgy in the room, didn't drink his tea, was only too eager to pack up his tools and be gone.

The next thing was a jagged incision gouged in the headboard of Peter's bed just inches from where his head had lain in feverish dreams. It got him another telling off from his mum. Later in the day, when he was working on a Heinkel 111, his dad came in. He cleared his throat, took an unconvincing interest in the model's retractable undercarriage, and then suggested Peter should surrender his craft knives overnight.

'What?'

'You can have them back in the morning. It's just your mum's worried in case you hurt yourself in the night.'

'You think I'm, like, sleeping with a knife in my hand? Is that what you think?'

The knives went into safekeeping for the night. But pens were still at large on Peter's table. In the middle of the night there was a loud yell as Peter was thrown bodily from his bed. His mum tried to come in, but Peter slammed the door to stop her and shouted he was all right. In the morning there was writing on the walls, in black and red. The words, even the letters, were hard to make out. Peter was scrubbing them with kitchen roll when his mum came in.

'O Peter! What are we going to do with you?'

When she stepped towards him the carpet was so waterlogged that she felt its chill dampness soak through her slipper.

'It wasn't me, Mum.'

'Well, who was it then?'

'How should I know?' He hesitated, then said in a quiet voice, 'It's like there's something's trying to communicate.'

'Well, that's a fine story' – and out she stamped. She didn't want to consider the possibility there was something wrong with her boy; really wrong, like in the head. Her husband said, 'It's probably just his age – the hormones, the peer pressure, the stress of schoolwork.'

'But he's not at school! It's the summer holidays!'

Another plumber was called in to investigate the water still streaming up the walls. Surely there must be a leak! But the plumber couldn't find it. He was sweating and shivering at the same time while he worked. When Peter came in, the plumber backed away nervously and kicked over his tea. He muttered something about another job and left without getting paid.

Then one night Peter woke in the small hours and saw something small and pale hovering a few inches above the footboard of the bed. There was just enough moonlight though the curtains to make it out: the little white hand of a young child. It seemed unconnected to any arm or sleeve; its wrist simply merged with the shadows.

As Peter watched, the hand slowly grew. It got as large as his own. It grew larger yet, became the hand of a young man. Its flesh thickened, became muscular, darker in complexion. Hairs sprouted on the back of it, grew denser and darker. The lines deepened round the knuckles. The veins became prominent. Liver spots mottled the skin. The hand became bonier, wrinklier, changing ever faster. The hairs turned grey. The veins bunched dark and wormlike. The flesh was falling away, the nails yellow and clawlike, the joints gnarled, the whole thing shrivelling to skeletal bones and leathery blotched skin.

At the moment when Peter's terror was about to find voice he heard from the shadows another voice speak.

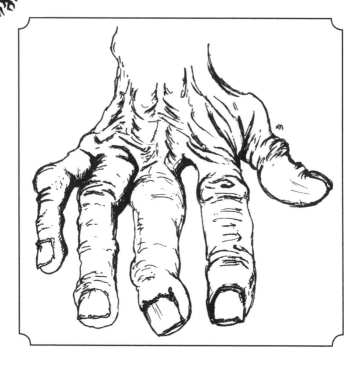

Then he did scream. His parents came running and found him sitting up in bed, soaked in sweat, hair standing on end, eyes jutting from their sockets, his smooth young hand raised, trembling, pointing to the end of the bed.

'What is it?' cried his mum – 'What's the matter?' – as she threw her arms round him and held him close in the way she'd used to do.

'Th-that hand!' stammered the boy. 'The v-voice!'

'What voice?' said Mr Rickett.

'The voice I heard in the dark.'

'What did it say?'

'It said … "All thesem years! All thesem years I been shut up here right!"' As Peter spoke, his voice was inflected by another one, older, hoarser, and ripe with the Cotswold accent rarely heard any more. '"What were it for the sake on, I ask ee? Te-unt as ee wantst to end up, locked up here right and no way out."'

'Who *are* you?' cried Mr Rickett with sudden inspiration.

"'I be one of they as did build this house. Aye, a good few housen I did build.'"

A moment later the lad was himself again and trembling in his mother's arms. Mr Rickett didn't know what to think except that plainly there was an untoward relation between his son and this house. His instinct was they should flee. The summer was already well advanced. Most holiday lets were long booked up, but after a dozen phone calls he struck lucky with a cottage in Devon that had just had a cancellation.

It was in a tiny hamlet, with a couple of farmhouses, a church, a vicarage. There were trees, birdsong, late summer flowers, and glorious gorse blossom on the moors. Yet even here Peter's night-time disturbances continued: tapping sounds, moving furniture, disarrayed bedclothes, moisture on the walls. The Ricketts were at their wits' end. Whatever was wrong was *in their son*!

Their third day there was a Sunday. They weren't regular churchgoers but they went to the church that morning, a tense little row of three in the rearmost pew, away from the old ladies sitting near the front so they could hear. The vicar was a wise old hand, though he'd been put out to pasture with this dwindling congregation. He knew that the family at the back were there for a reason. He took them to the vicarage for coffee afterwards and listened while Mr Rickett explained, and Peter sat in sullen silence, and his mother kept interrupting to say there was nothing wrong with him.

Over the next few days there followed a series of interviews. I won't call it an exorcism; that wasn't the vicar's style. His manner of speech and prayer was wheedling and gentle. To the parents sitting a few pews away he seemed sometimes to be addressing their son and sometimes someone else.

At last they heard him say, 'There is a way onward, you know. You need not be trapped for ever.'

From the boy's lips came a gruff Cotswold gargle.

'This old church is a restful place,' said the vicar. 'Think of it as somewhere to pause, catch your breath – as it were – before you move on.'

So the vicar's coaxing continued, till at last the boy vented a great sigh and there was a flurry of movement all around – a flapping of the altar cloth, a riffling of the pages of the Bible on the lectern, a rattling of doors and windows.

Peter looked dazed but at peace. When they got home to Stow the disturbances did not resume. Peter resumed work on his Airfix models and now and again he looked out at the old workhouse and wondered about all that had happened to him. He couldn't remember what words he'd uttered in that strange aged voice. But his father could.

Mr Rickett made some enquiries. He discovered that one of the men who'd built their house had ended up in the workhouse, or 'Public Assistance Institution' as it was by then, and died there in 1943, exactly twenty years before the date – one day after Peter's birthday – that Peter first heard the tapping in the wardrobe. As Peter built his Spitfires and Hurricanes, his Heinkels and Messerschmitts, and watched out of his window, he thought of an old man fading away in body and mind and trapped in a high-walled prison while the air-raid sirens wailed and flights of German bombers grumbled overhead.

20

THE CHRISTMAS GHOST

I t was Christmas Day in Gloucester, a dreary grey morning, the kind when most people would prefer to be huddling in front of a fire, opening presents and drinking eggnog. A few people, however, were making their way down from the flats nearby to the little church of St Mary de Lode, just outside the cathedral precinct, for the nine o'clock service. The little room at the west end of the church had been decorated with a tree and lots of tinsel, and a table was laid with a tea urn, mugs, coffee, and biscuits for after the service. It looked very jolly, but as people entered they drew up the collars of their coats and shivered.

'It's freezing in here.'

'Hope the heating hasn't broken.'

'Hope it's not as cold in the church, else our bums'll freeze to the pews!'

But inside the church it was warm and the congregation soon forgot about the cold in the church room.

When everyone was settled, the vicar came in, walked up the aisle, and surveyed her congregation with some satisfaction. Every year she feared that this service would be empty, with the temptation of the ten o'clock service next door at the cathedral, but here they were, her loyal little flock.

She was just about to start when she noticed that something strange was happening to doors to the church room: a slight

blurring of the surface of the wood. Her first thought was that her eyes must be watering, but everything else in the church remained crystal clear. As she watched, a seeping dark mass began to appear in front of the doors. It grew and swelled and then coalesced into a smoky figure clad in a long, dark, hooded cloak. People at the back of the church began to shiver as if they were cold, but none of them seemed aware that anything was amiss.

The vicar stared in shock. She would have bolted straight out the door if the apparition were not there blocking the way. She took a deep breath and glanced down at the floor to steady herself. She remembered then a tale an old parishioner had told her when she first started at St Mary's. She realised what this apparition was and what she had to do.

As she looked up, the sun came out and light flooded through the windows. In the bright sunlight the figure at the back of the church was almost impossible to see. Up the steps to the pulpit went the vicar; there she pushed aside her sermon notes and forced a smile for her puzzled congregation.

'Welcome,' she said, fixing her gaze on the apparition, 'on this Christmas morning.' And with her words the hooded figure began to fade.

'Before we have the first hymn I'd like to begin by telling you a story. You all know that this church is old – maybe the oldest foundation in Britain, going right back to Roman times. Well, this story isn't that old, but it's from a long time ago, when things were very different in the Church. Back in the fourteenth century there were those who believed the Church was corrupt, venal, and controlled by secular powers. The Pope had even been thrown out of Rome, and seven of the popes had to rule – if you can call it that – from Avignon in France. Here in England there was one man, an Oxford scholar called John Wycliffe, who called out for reform, and many priests secretly agreed with him – including, possibly, the vicar of St Mary's.

'In 1377 the Pope, Gregory XI, got back to Rome. He immediately began issuing papal bulls. All the ones that came to England were about Wycliffe – and how he should be stopped. The vicar of St Mary's decided he couldn't stand for that. He decided to go to Rome and petition the Pope. His parishioners begged him not to go.

'"Where will we go?" they cried. "Who will marry us? Who will baptise our babies, say Mass for us, and bury our dead?"

'The priest reassured them they would be looked after at the other churches in Gloucester. He insisted he had to go and told them, "I swear to you that I will be back to celebrate midnight mass with you on Christmas Eve. Wait for me. I swear I will be there."

'There was nothing the parishioners could do, and soon the priest set off on his journey. Nowadays it takes – what? – two hours to get to Rome by plane. It took a lot longer then. Even the journey to Dover was long and arduous. After his passage across the Channel the priest travelled southwards through France on foot. He joined a band of pilgrims to make the perilous crossing through the Alps, teetering along mountain paths. Once in Italy, there was a long walk to Rome with only his not very good Latin to help him.

'So it was months after leaving Gloucester that he arrived in Rome in the blazing summer heat. He didn't have to wait long to be granted an audience with Pope Gregory, but as soon as he saw the Pope he knew his pleas would fall on deaf ears. The Pope was an old man, ill, irascible, and not inclined to listen to anyone. Still, the priest bravely made his case for Wycliffe and his ideas, explaining how good it would be to see the Church in England reformed and to have a Bible in English for all to understand.

'The Pope got angry and waved him away. "Get back to your congregation, you impudent priest!" he cried. "Be thankful I don't write a bull against you!"

'The priest had no choice but to turn around and go home, defeated. He realised, too, that if he wanted to fulfil his promise to his flock to be home for Christmas he had to set off straight away. He made it through the Alps just as the first snow showers were falling in the mountains. As quickly as he could, he journeyed back through France. He reached Calais in time to secure one of the last passages across the Channel at the beginning of December.

'Meanwhile, back here in Gloucester, things were not going well for his parishioners. They hadn't been welcomed in the other parishes. Weddings were held too late for coming babies, and sometimes christenings came too late as well. The dead languished for days before burial. Confessions went unheard. Many parishioners had given up going to church at all.

'The elders of the parish tried to keep people's spirits up, saying, "Our priest promised he'd be home for Christmas, and so he shall be."

'When December arrived and there was no sign of the priest the people's hearts sank even further and they began to mutter that he wasn't coming back at all.

'"Nonsense," said the elders. "He said he was coming, and so he shall, even if it takes him till midnight on Christmas Eve. And we will be there to welcome him."

'Christmas week came, and still the priest hadn't returned, yet the elders resolutely gathered everyone together and unlocked the long-neglected church. It was in a filthy state; all that week they swept and scrubbed and cleaned. They decorated the walls with greenery and set new candles in the sconces. By Christmas Eve everything was ready, and it was a hopeful congregation that made their way down to the church to celebrate Christ's birth. But when they arrived the church was still shrouded in darkness.

'"He's never coming back!" someone cried.

'"He may still come," said one of the elders, his voice hesitant. Then stronger: "And we must be here to welcome him!"

'They trooped into the church and lit the candles. Then they waited, singing carols to cheer them in the winter chill.

'Just before midnight the wind suddenly picked up. It rattled the roof beams and whistled through the gaps in the window glass. It wuthered under the door, rustled the greenery, and flickered the candles. The church grew colder and colder. One by one the voices of the singers died away until there was only the sound of the wind howling around the church.

'Then, with a crash, the west door banged open. Half the candles blew out, smothering the place in darkness. As the people's eyes adjusted, someone cried out, "He's here!" Standing in the doorway was the unmistakable figure of their priest, shrouded in his long dark cloak. Filled with joy even in the gloom, they called out welcomes to him.

'He didn't answer, just walked up the aisle. Their words of welcome faltered. Silently he went to stand at the altar. His shoes made no sound on the floor. But as he began to speak the Latin words they were swept away into the familiar liturgy. Only a few noticed that his voice sounded strange and hollow.

'"He sounds like he's talking from the bottom of the sea," one man murmured to his neighbour, but he was quickly shushed.

'Soon the Mass was done and they all raised their voices as he led them in song to welcome in Christ's birth – just as the bells of the abbey next door rang out to mark the beginning of Christmas Day. Moments later their own bells joined them. As the priest walked back down the aisle, seeming to glide in the semi-darkness, his parishioners called out again how pleased they were to see him. He didn't answer them. In the blink of an eye he disappeared into the gloom at the west end.

'In a little while, some of them went to ask him about his journey; but he was nowhere to be seen. They took up the remaining candles and searched the church. When they still couldn't find him they spilled out into the night, calling his name as they walked around the building.

'Past the east end they saw a figure in a long cloak, carrying a lantern, coming towards them from the abbey gatehouse. As he approached they realised he wasn't their priest but one of the monks from the abbey.

'"Are you the people of St Mary's?" he called. "I'm afraid we had some news come for you this evening. We thought to wait until tomorrow, but when we saw you here we thought it best to tell you now. A messenger came today from Dover with word of your priest. There was a storm at sea a week or so back, and I'm very sorry to say that the ship on which he was sailing was lost with all souls."

'"But that can't be!" cried someone. "He was here – just now. He took the Mass for us. There must be some mistake."

'The monk shook his head. "There's no mistake. Whoever took your Mass, it wasn't your priest. You best all go home now, and after the holiday we shall help you with the arrangements."

'With that he turned and went back to the abbey. The parishioners stared at each other. One by one, they realised what must have happened and what they had seen in the church. Their priest had kept his promise. He had come back to them, but from further away than any could have imagined. He had come all the way from heaven itself.'

The vicar smiled down at her flock in the warm sunny church. They looked surprised at the story, as well they might. They'd be even more surprised if they knew what she had seen.

'The parishioner who told me the tale said that that priest still comes back sometimes,' she went on. 'Just to check that Christmas services are still being held. When he comes it is always a good year for the parish. Happy Christmas everyone! It looks like it will be a good year!' She smiled again when she saw the startled looks on their faces. 'May we all be able to keep our promises with such faith as that lost parish priest from long ago.'

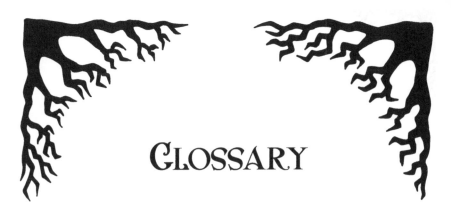

GLOSSARY

ain't . . . . hasn't
allus . . . . always

bent . . . . isn't
besom . . . . woman
bugaboo . . . . ghost
bull . . . . papal edict

counter hopper . . . . shop assistant
curflummox . . . . with a heavy fall

ee . . . . you

firedamp . . . . explosive gas that forms in mines

gadjo . . . . non-Roma
gadular . . . . gadulka player
gadulka . . . . bowed stringed instrument
                                              from Bulgaria
gapesnatch . . . . fool

here right . . . . in this very place
housen . . . . houses

lagged . . . . fatigued

nanimal . . . . animal
nation . . . . very
neddy . . . . donkey

ourn . . . . ours

preceptor . . . . head of a preceptory
preceptory . . . . community of monastic knights

solar . . . . upper chamber in medieval house

te-unt . . . . it isn't
thesem . . . . these
tump . . . . small rounded hill
tympanum . . . . space within an arch and above
                                       a doorway

Ursar . . . . Roma bear handler from Romania
                                       or Bulgaria

ware . . . . beware
we'm . . . . we are
Whitechapel cart . . . . light two-wheeled sprung cart

yent . . . . isn't
yere . . . . here
yud . . . . head

Bibliography

Brooks, J.A., *Ghosts and Witches of the Cotswolds* (Jarrold, 1981)

Clark, K., *The Ghosts of Gloucestershire* (Redcliffe, 1993)

Douglas-Home, J., *Violet: Life and Loves of Violet Gordon Woodhouse* (Harvill, 1996)

Fry, E. & Harvey, R., *Haunted Gloucester* (Tempus, 2004)

Jewson, N., *By Chance I Did Rove* (Gryffon, 1986)

Law, S., *Ghosts of the Forest of Dean* (Douglas McLean, 2011)

Leech, J., *Brief Romances from Bristol History* (William George, 1884)

Le'Queux, S., *Haunted Bristol* (Tempus, 2004)

Lewis-Jones, J., *Folklore of the Cotswolds* (Tempus, 2003)

Macer-Wright, D., *The Hauntings of Littledean Hall* (Douglas McLean, 2012)

Massingham, H.J., *Shepherd's Country: A Record of the Crafts and People of the Hills* (Chapman & Hall, 1938)

Matthews, R., *Haunted Gloucestershire* (Logaston Press, 2006)

Meredith, B., *The Haunted Cotswolds* (Reardon, 1999)

Mountjoy, T., *The Life, Labours and Deliverances of a Forest of Dean Collier* (A. Chilver, 1887)

National Trust, *Snowshill Manor and Garden* (2010)

Palmer, R., *The Folklore of Gloucestershire* (Westcountry Books, 1994)

Parkinson, D.J. et al., 'Headless Black Dog', *Mysterious Britain & Ireland* (online, 2008)

Partridge, J.B., 'Cotswold Place-Lore and Customs', *Folklore*, Vol. 23, No. 3 (1912)

Smith, B., *Tales of Old Gloucestershire* (Countryside Books, 1987)

Turner, M., *Folklore and Mysteries of the Cotswolds* (Robert Hale, 1993)

Turner, M., *Mysterious Gloucestershire* (The History Press, 2011)

Westwood, J. & Simpson, J., *The Lore of the Land* (Penguin, 2006)

White, D., *Haunted Cotswolds* (The History Press, 2010)

Williams, A., *Lays and Legends of Gloucestershire* (Kent, 1878)

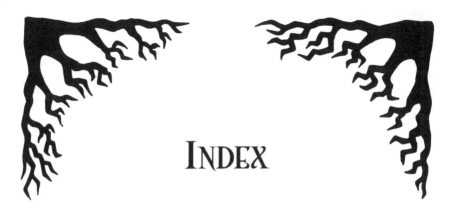

INDEX

ABOUT THE AUTHORS

ANTHONY NANSON and KIRSTY HARTSIOTIS are popular Stroud-based storytellers. Separately and together in the company Fire Springs, they have performed widely in Britain and beyond. Anthony teaches creative writing at Bath Spa University and is the author of *Gloucestershire Folk Tales*, *Exotic Excursions*, *Storytelling and Ecology*, *Words of Re-enchantment*, and the novel *Deep Time* and also co-editor of *Storytelling for a Greener World*. Kirsty is the author of *Wiltshire Folk Tales* and *Suffolk Folk Tales* and combines storytelling and writing with work as a museum curator in Cheltenham.

Find out more at:
www.anthonynanson.co.uk
www.kirstyhartsiotis.co.uk

Also from The History Press

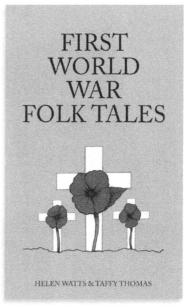

Find this title and more at
www.thehistorypress.co.uk

Also from The History Press

More Spooky Books

Society *for* Storytelling

Since 1993, the Society for Storytelling has championed the art of oral storytelling and the benefits it can provide – such as improving memory more than rote learning, promoting healing by stimulating the release of neuropeptides, or simply great entertainment! Storytellers, enthusiasts and academics support and are supported by this registered charity to ensure the art is nurtured and developed throughout the UK.

Many activities of the Society are available to all, such as locating storytellers on the Society website, taking part in our annual National Storytelling Week at the start of every February, purchasing our quarterly magazine *Storylines*, or attending our Annual Gathering – a chance to revel in engaging performances, inspiring workshops, and the company of like-minded people.

You can also become a member of the Society to support the work we do. In return, you receive free access to *Storylines*, discounted tickets to the Annual Gathering and other storytelling events, the opportunity to join our mentorship scheme for new storytellers, and more. Among our great deals for members is a 30% discount off titles in the *Folk Tales* series from The History Press website.

For more information, including how to join, please visit

www.sfs.org.uk